Also by Eric Wright

BURIED IN STONE

· IN ·

A MEL PICKETT MYSTERY

ERIC WRIGHT

SCRIBNER

New York   London   Toronto   Sydney   Tokyo   Singapore

SCRIBNER
Rockefeller Center
1230 Avenue of the Americas
New York, NY 10020

Copyright © 1995 by Eric Wright
All rights reserved,
including the right of reproduction in whole
of in part in any form.

SCRIBNR and design are trademarks of Simon & Schuster Inc.

Designed by Erich Hobbing

Manufactured in the United States of America

10 9 8 7 6 5 4 3 2 1

Library of Congress Cataloging-In-Publication Data
Wright, Eric, 1929-
Buried in stone: a Mel Pickett mystery/Eric Wright.
p.   cm.
I.   Title
PR919.3W66B8   1996
813'.54-dc20   95-34.97   CIP

ISBN: 0-7432-0514-6

for Jack Batten

ONE

Eleven-thirty. Mel Pickett opened the door of his tiny refrigerator to see what he had left to eat. It was too soon for lunch, but he had done a good morning's work, and he was entitled to see what he might look forward to. He counted half a barbecued chicken, some liverwurst, a bit of potato salad, and a slab of Canadian Gouda. A container on top of the refrigerator yielded two rolls of Italian bread and four butter tarts. And he still had three bottles of Upper Canada Point Nine (de-alcoholized) Ale, his latest attempt to find something to drink at noon that would taste like beer but would not leave him sluggish all afternoon. Pickett was sixty-five, and the older he got the less booze it took to send him into a light doze. The problem was just as serious as Alzheimer's, impotence, angina, crumbling bones, receding gums, and all the other ills old flesh is heir to.

Satisfied with his inventory, he closed the door of the fridge and heated a cup of old tea in the microwave, deciding he could manage another hour's work before he ate.

Pickett was a retired Toronto policeman, a widower with no responsibilities. He was spending the weekend, and perhaps the rest of the week, with Willis, his tiny, foolish-looking dog, in a cabin that he had built on a piece of land just outside Larch River, a town 150 miles north of Toronto. The lot he had bought had nothing much to recommend it. It lay between the town and the river, too far from the town to be useful to a villager and too far from the river to be attractive to an outsider wanting to build a summer cottage; in fact, useless for anything except what Pickett wanted it for, to build a cabin just to see if he could do it, and it had been for sale for a long time before he found it. The land did rise slightly in the center of the lot, where he had built the cabin, so that sitting on his porch he had—not exactly a view but a sense of space. And near the edge of the lot a swamp gave way to a pond big enough to support two otters. Otherwise it was simply five acres of undeveloped bush, with large patches of rock showing through the thin covering of earth.

After a lifetime of careful saving, waiting for the Great Depression of his childhood to return, Pickett had arrived at his present age with a comfortable pension, seventy-five thousand dollars in Canada Savings Bonds, a few stocks, about fifty thousand in cash, and a small mortgage-free house in Toronto. When his wife died, he converted the house into two apartments, and the rent from the second floor more than covered the upkeep on the house. His only toy was a new Volvo station wagon. Thus Pickett, by Micawber's definition, was a very rich man, certainly rich enough to indulge the whim of building his own log cabin.

His desire to build a cabin began with the discovery

of a photograph of his great-grandfather, a short, bald, grinning, rascally looking character with three or four teeth, standing beside the cabin he had built, holding his ax. Pickett was not trying to rediscover his roots by imitating him. Nor was he drawn to the project in any spirit of historical romanticism, such as prompts people to sail across the Atlantic in a replica of the *Mayflower*. He just wanted to solve the construction problems involved. He was a good carpenter—he had done all the renovations on his own house—and the idea of building a cabin had come along just at a time when he needed a project. Although he went to Florida for a few weeks every winter when he had had enough snow, he had no desire to live there, to join the hordes of old Canadians creaking in the sun. He still needed work to do.

He had chosen to build in the cottage country of central Ontario because there was still plenty of cheap undeveloped land there. Pickett had grown up in southwest Ontario, in country that had been developed for a hundred years, and he was surprised at first at what he found when he went north looking for a site. Very few of the towns of cottage country are pretty; they have grown by serving the needs of the summer trade, and even at the height of the season they have a temporary feel, as if they are waiting to dismantle themselves for the winter, like circuses. Larch River looked more permanent than most. The town had been there before the district became vacation land, and though part of it was strung out along the highway in the form of fast-food outlets and live bait shops to attract the passing trade, there was an older part that lay east, off the highway, eight or ten streets of houses mixed with small businesses. On the west side, a small road led past a sawmill to the town beach, but hardly any of the thousands of people who drove the highway every weekend knew of it because there was no signpost.

It took Pickett some time to realize the nature of the community he had chosen to buy into. When he thought about it at all, he assumed that beyond the tourists the town serviced the area's—what? Farmers? He hadn't actually seen any farms but they were probably around somewhere. As his knowledge grew, so did his curiosity, and he learned that there was only one significant employer in the area, the lumber mill, which in a way kept Larch River true to its origins. There was also a canoe builder, who employed a dozen people, a large chicken farm, and several other assorted enterprises, including a bakery that supplied fresh bread to the whole area, but it was the lumber mill that primed the local pump. A significant fragment of the population was made up of commuters, mainly younger people who had grown up in Larch River and still lived at home but worked in Sweetwater, eight miles to the south, a town big enough to contain government offices and a detachment of the Ontario Provincial Police. And a final fragment of the population was made up of retired people, both locals and people who had come to Larch River as if it were Florida. More and more these outside people could be heard explaining that the charm of places like Larch River to them was that here they could still find the Ontario they grew up in, by which they meant that, so far, the townspeople were all a familiar white.

Gradually Pickett absorbed some idea of the town and its history, which was simple and typical. It had started as a lumbering town; then, after the first-growth timber had been shaved off, it became an agricultural community as the homesteads turned into established farms. Now there were only two working farms left as the farmers sold out to investment bankers looking for a hobby for the present and an investment for the future, and to real estate developers. So far Larch River had managed to postpone becoming a purely tourist town, but inevitably as the pressure of population increased in Toronto it would be discovered by the people who could not afford the Georgian Bay or Muskoka.

It had been cold in the night, but now it was already too warm for a jacket. Pickett took his tea outside to enjoy the last of the summer sun; he gave Willis a biscuit to help her over her disappointment that the opening of the fridge had not ushered in lunch.

Outside, the landscape announced the coming of fall, a blaze of red and yellow foliage under a clear blue sky. As he sat down, a Volkswagen Golf turned onto his land from the county road, stopping in front of the porch. Willis rushed down the steps to bark at the visitors, and a man in his late twenties got out, established that Willis was harmless, and came to where Pickett was standing on the porch. Pickett could see a woman in the passenger seat of the car, a blonde, staring straight ahead, but he could not see her face because the angle at which the sun met the windshield created a dazzling patch of light. He got ready to give the man directions, wondering how they could have got lost. They had come along the only road that led up from the bridge over the river—and then he saw, before the man reached him, that something was wrong.

"I'm afraid we have rather an emergency on our hands," the man said.

His speech and posture were unnaturally stylized, as if he was having trouble choosing the right level of discourse for addressing Pickett. He seemed vaguely familiar, but he was obviously not a local man, being curiously dressed for a Sunday morning drive, or walk, or whatever they had been doing. Above a pair of brand-new jeans, he wore a white dress shirt, buttoned to the neck without a tie, and a tweed jacket. His brown dress shoes were edged with mud and fragments of leaves. He looked as if he had put on whatever had come to hand when a fire alarm sounded.

"You lost?" Pickett asked.

"Not exactly. Look, I rather think we've met, you and I. You will perhaps remember my . . ." He turned as if to avoid choosing a term to apply to the woman in the car.

The door of the car opened and the woman got out and came toward them. She walked carefully, as if she couldn't see very well. Her face was white, and as she got closer, her throat started to convulse. "Mr. Pickett," she said. "Mel."

Pickett said, "Eliza?" Then, to the man, "Hold on to her, quick. She's going to fall."

The man just managed to get his arm around her shoulders as she turned and vomited into the weeds beside the path. Pickett went into the house for a box of tissues, getting a handful to her as she straightened up. She thanked him without looking up, and turned to the man. "Why didn't you stop me?" she said in a small voice full of misery. "You didn't try to stop me."

"I think you insisted, Eliza, but we can conduct the . . . we can discuss it later. At this moment . . ."

"You should've stopped me," she repeated, and turned to be sick again.

Pickett said, "Let's get her inside." He picked up the dog and took the woman by the elbow, leading the couple into the house. Inside, he sat her on the couch. "Lie down when you think it's safe," he said. The young woman, still waiting with her head bent to see if she had finished throwing up, acknowledged the instruction with a tiny hand gesture, then looked up and gave Pickett a small smile. He smiled back. "Hi," he said.

The man walked to the door, jamming his hands in his jacket pockets, then immediately took them out, as if looking for the right instinct to guide him.

"Tell him now, Dennis," the woman said. She looked to either side of her and collected two cushions, which she piled up at one end of the couch. She squeezed off her loafers then, and slowly revolved so that she was sitting sideways with her legs outstretched.

"You want to lie down now?" Pickett asked.

"Not yet." Again she went very white, but this time her color began to return immediately.

"Tell me in a minute," Pickett said. He shook the teapot and found enough left, which he heated and mixed with a lot of cream and three spoonfuls of sugar.

She took it from him and sipped it, making a face at the sweetness, but finished the cup.

"More?" Pickett asked.

She nodded, holding out the cup.

He plugged in the kettle and put some fresh tea bags into the pot. "You want some?" he asked the man.

The man said, "Yes. It seems to have helped her. The sugar settles the stomach, no doubt?"

The woman made a gesture as if to quiet him.

"The sugar's for the shock," Pickett said. "It looks as if it was considerable." He wondered what had happened down by the river, what they had seen, and why this character seemed like a refugee from *Masterpiece Theatre*.

"Ah."

The woman shivered slightly and Pickett disappeared into the bedroom and came out with a sheepskin jacket, which she pulled around her, although it was only slightly cooler in the cabin than outside, and she seemed adequately dressed in blue jeans and a woollen bush shirt.

No one said anything else until Pickett had poured them all more tea. Willis jumped on to the woman's lap, causing her to recoil in timidity. Pickett lifted the dog off and tucked it under his arm. He took a chair and gestured toward another, but the man remained standing, leaning against the doorpost. Pickett wondered when, if ever, he was going to express concern or try to comfort the woman.

"We—er—came across a body," the man said. "My name's Dennis Corning, by the way. As I say, I think we have met. Eliza you know, of course. Eliza Pollock."

Corning seemed to want to show his self-control, his ability to cope with the discovery of the body, but his attempt at composure was belied by the pale face and the slightly jerky speech, which, Pickett now realized, was what had reminded him of a certain kind of acting.

Pickett nodded. "Where?"

"At the play rehearsals."

"I know where I met Eliza, and you. I meant this body."

"Right. Yes. Upon the trail that runs behind the cottages across the river. Do you know these parts?"

"I know that trail," Pickett said. "I've walked along it. With the dog."

Corning said, "There's a bit of flat rock about half a mile in. On one side there's a deep crack about three or four feet wide where the rock split when the original glacier passed by, I imagine. The far side of the crack is a few feet lower, so the flat rock is like a little cliff over a gully about six feet deep. Do you follow? The body was in the gully. It's not going to go away."

"Did you just come across it, walking by?"

"We stopped to take a rest and I walked over to take a look in the crevasse." He seemed momentarily embarrassed.

Pickett wondered how secluded the spot was, how long the body had been there. "More tea?" he asked them both. "We'd better phone Lyman Caxton directly."

"And who is Lyman Caxton?"

"He's the chief of police, the town cop. There's just the one."

"Ah, yes, I remember my aunt speaking of him. Look,

I wonder, could you look after it, perhaps? I'll give you our address." The man began searching his pockets.

Eliza interrrupted him. "For God's sake, of course he can't, Dennis. You and I will have to report it."

"You found it, it's yours until you report it," Pickett agreed, wondering where Eliza, whom he liked a lot, had found this guy. He recognized the type: the man belonged to that group of the population who when confronted with a serious misery—a traffic accident, say, or a motorist alone with a boiling radiator as the fog rolls over Dartmoor—do not instinctively stop to help; rather they instinctively check their watches, realizing that their own schedule is in danger of being thrown off. The people with bad instincts.

Pickett went into his bedroom to make the phone call and sat on his bed to think. Her name was Eliza Pollock, and she was a freelance book editor, if he remembered the term right, and the director of the local amateur dramatic group, into which, to his pleased surprise, she had co-opted Pickett as the stage carpenter. Dennis Corning was a Toronto university professor who worked only two days a week in the winter and not at all in the summer, so they lived in Larch River while he did something else. What else could Pickett remember? Corning had inherited the house from a relative, and he and Eliza lived there most of the time, but he also had a bachelor apartment in Toronto. They weren't married. What else? Corning was writing a film script, that was it. Something about a historical incident that took place in the area about the time of the great Irish potato famine. Involving someone accused of murder.

Behind him, in the main room, a small, whispered squabble broke out. He made the phone call. When he returned, Corning looked sullen and Eliza looked depressed.

"He's expecting us in fifteen minutes," Pickett reported. "Finish your tea and we'll go up."

Corning stood. "No need for Eliza to go, is there? Surely I can take care of it?"

Pickett saw that Corning had been made aware, temporarily at least, that it was time to think of others. Or at any rate, to remember his manners.

"She can rest here for now," he agreed. "Caxton will want a statement later on, but you and I can go up now."

She smiled at him gratefully and swung her legs to the floor, tried to stand, and then sat down. "Not quite," she said. "Not quite." She pulled the jacket close.

CHAPTER 2

Lyman Caxton was Larch River's chief of police, one of the very few one-man police forces left in Ontario. Caxton had appeared quite early, while the cabin was still in the planning stage. Pickett had told no one in the town of his own background, but when he saw the look of bright discovery on Caxton's face as the police chief got out of his car in front of Pickett's cabin one morning, he knew he was about to be claimed as a colleague. One of Pickett's old buddies in the Bail and Parole unit in Toronto had been inquiring after him to let him know about the funeral of another colleague, had tracked him down to Larch River, and had asked the police chief to relay the message.

After that, Caxton called whenever Pickett was in residence; Caxton had never been a policeman before he was appointed chief in Larch River, and he liked talking police talk to Pickett, whom he admired enormously. Pickett, in his turn, at first thought Caxton to be something of a fool, but soon began to appreciate another side of the chief, what he thought of as Caxton's "country" side. Caxton was apparently wholly and comfortably in charge of the physical world. He understood car

engines, boilers, septic tank systems, pumps, and everything else mechanical with an instinct that he took no
pride in whatsoever. And he was just as much at home
in the natural world. Pickett very early became used to
Caxton pointing out the signs of raccoons or foxes or
some other creature that had passed across Pickett's
land, signs that Pickett often couldn't see a second time
after he had momentarily taken his eyes off them. Later,
when he knew Caxton better, it seemed to Pickett that
Caxton's view of the natural world included its human
inhabitants. He automatically registered the external
behavior of all the creatures he met and was immediately aware when a person or animal behaved oddly, as
if he were always on the alert for rabies.

What drew the two men together, then, was a mutual
admiration: Pickett knew all about being a cop, and
Caxton (or so it seemed to Pickett) knew everything
else. And Caxton was a police buff. In landing the job at
Larch River he had satisfied a major childhood desire,
and in Pickett he found his idol, a man who had worked
as an investigator in the homicide branch of the Toronto
police. Every time they met, Caxton had a new question
for Pickett, and if they spent an hour together, Pickett
was sure to spend five minutes explaining police technique. Thus when Caxton appeared while Pickett was
building the cabin, Pickett usually had a construction
problem for Caxton to solve in exchange for his newly
thought up question about fingerprints or bloodstains.

It was useful to have the chief on his side. Very early
in their relationship Pickett had some tools, a new
chain saw among them, stolen from his little trailer

while he was in the city. He told Caxton the next time he called. Caxton looked around the trailer, nodded, and said, "It was one of the locals. I'll see what I can find out."

"How do you know it was a local?"

"They took the useful stuff, the saw and the good tools. But they didn't take your heater, though that's worth money, or your little fridge there. You might need them, see, to survive. But you can manage without a saw until you can buy another one. The locals think you're worth a few bucks."

Caxton never found the saw or who took it, but no one ever stole anything from Pickett again, and it took him no effort to realize why.

The police chief was waiting for them on the steps of his house. Caxton was a big man with a more or less permanent smile on a round, meaty face. Mainly because of his haircut—short on the back and sides and combed long across the top—he looked out of date, like a police chief from a thirties movie.

He waited for them to approach the steps. "Hi, Mel," he called. "I was hoping to get my storms up, but that'll have to wait, I guess."

"This is Dennis Corning," Pickett said.

"Dennis," Caxton said, putting his hand out. "Come on in, Dennis. You too, Mel," he added, winking, making a little joke out of the possibility that Pickett might not have felt himself included in the invitation. He led the way inside. "Hey, Dennis. Aren't you Dinah Stuckey's nephew?"

"She left me her house when she died."

"That's what I heard. Going to be living here now, are you?"

Pickett, seeing the irritation on Corning's face at Caxton's inappropriate attempts to be sociable, said, "It was Mr. Corning and the lady he was with who found the body, not me, Lyman."

Caxton waited a long time to respond, showing he had got the message, looking squarely at Corning. "Who's the lady?" he asked. "Let's sit down." He put on his glasses.

"Her name is Eliza Pollock."

Caxton wrote this down and turned to look at Pickett. "Where is she now?"

"We left her at my place. She was feeling rocky."

"I'll have to interview her separately. Where is the body?" He looked over his glasses out the window as if he expected to see it propped up in the back of Pickett's car.

"On the trail up behind the row of cottages."

"Anyone we know?" Caxton asked Pickett.

"I haven't seen it."

"A man?" Caxton asked Corning.

"I think so. Pants. Yes. Work boots. But he was unrecognizable. Animals, I would think. I didn't look for long."

"Color of hair?"

"Easy!" Pickett warned, as Corning's face went white.

Caxton moved quickly across the room and caught the man as he tottered. He laid him down on the couch and went into the bedroom for a pillow and comforter. When he had covered Corning, he beckoned Pickett out of the room. "Delayed reaction," he said, authoritatively. "I'll get Dr. Kuntz to come over. I saw him pull up to the house a few minutes ago. You go back to the girl. I'll be along soon. I know that place on the trail. Maybe you and I could take a look? I know all those cottagers, though I guess it's probably a stranger or there would have been a report. I ain't heard of anybody missing." Now Caxton was getting excited. "I wonder how long it's been there. Last body we found had been there forty years, they said. Some poor bastard had just walked into the bush and fell down a hole. Didn't have any people to worry about him so he wasn't missed. No foul play that they could find. They found the skeleton last year when they were surveying up there." He began to load his pockets with items from the desk. "I'll pick you up in a little while, okay?"

Pickett sighed. "I'm retired." He put his hand up to deny what he had just said. "No, no. Sure. But it might take more than two of us to fetch it out."

"Depends. Probably have to bring in the OPP, anyway."

Pickett looked up, surprised. This sounded like a big leap. For some reason, he had been assuming that whoever it was had died in the bush, at worst had had an accident, fallen down drunk, perhaps. It had not yet occurred to him that the victim might have been murdered. "I think Dennis meant a bear had got to him."

Caxton shook his head and glanced through the doorway at Dennis Corning. "We don't have those kind of bears around here." He smiled. "They say some wolves were sighted along near that ravine last winter. I don't know. Probably a couple of dogs run wild. Anyway, one of us might have to stay with it." He tightened his belt. "We'll take a look, but there's bound to be an investigation. I'm not set up for that." He added, "I'll just check that Betty's all right. She's got flu or some damn thing. We usually get together Sunday afternoons. I told her I'd look in when I'd finished the storms. Now let's go see if we can make an ID."

Betty Cullen was Caxton's girlfriend in a relationship that went back to long before Pickett had arrived in town, but they maintained separate houses. "I'll wait for you at the cabin," Pickett said. He drove off to look after Eliza.

Half an hour later, Caxton appeared outside Pickett's door. He had changed from his Sunday afternoon clothes into his police chief's costume: khaki pants and shirt, badge, and what Pickett thought was a slightly silly pointed hat. His demeanor had changed, too. He looked harassed.

He's had a fight with his girl, Pickett thought, as he came out to the porch to meet Caxton. He put a finger to his lips. "She's got her eyes closed," he said.

"I've left Dennis to rest up, too," Caxton said. "The doctor said he'll be all right."

The door opened behind them. "Can I go over there now?" Eliza asked. She seemed to have recovered completely.

"Wait a bit," Caxton said. "He'll be okay in a bit. Let's

go, Mel. Oh, I'd better get your statement first." He took out his notebook and a ballpoint pen and looked at his wristwatch. "Now. When did you come across the body?"

When he had finished, he said, "These are just notes, really. I'll type this up later. Ready, Mel?"

Pickett could see that Caxton was sweating slightly, trying not to make a mistake. For a moment, he was afraid that the police chief would warn Eliza she mustn't leave town, but Caxton was impatient now to view the site, and trotted off to his car.

Pickett's cabin was served by a gravel road that ran southwest from the town, past his cabin, and then crossed the river by a one-lane steel bridge before continuing on to a summer cottage community on the shore of Otter Lake. Duck Lake and Otter Lake were actually two large swellings in the river. Duck Lake was close to the town and provided the beach; it was connected to Otter Lake to the south by a narrow strip of the river about a mile long. The swamp that lay between the town and Duck Lake also made the east bank of the river unsuitable for development, but half a dozen cottages had been built on the other bank.

The road turned south after it crossed the bridge, but at the foot of the bridge on the far side, the town had cleared and graveled a parking space and set out two picnic tables. There was no road to the cottages along the river shore. The owners kept boats at the marina on Duck Lake and came in by water.

The two men parked in the picnic space and started up the trail. Soon it climbed sharply away from the river as a gully developed that split the land and forced the trail higher. Very quickly they were high enough so that they were catching only an occasional glimpse of a cottage between the trees, and past the cottages the river formed a backdrop to the scene. Caxton led them straight to the spot on the trail that Eliza had described, and Pickett leaned against a birch tree as the police chief walked to the edge of the gully and dropped to his knees to peer down. Almost immediately he stood up again and walked back to sit down in the spot where Eliza and Corning had stopped. He put his head in his hands. Pickett wondered if Caxton had ever seen a dead body. Twenty years in the Department of Lands and Forests, then seven years in Larch River would not have produced many.

"I'll wait here," Pickett said. "You go do what you have to."

Caxton sniffed hard and shook his head as if to clear it. "I'll radio them from the car, then come back up, let you go home. Be fifteen minutes."

"Know who he is?"

"No face left. It's a mess." The sight of the body seemed to have astonished him, as if he had not expected death to look like that. He slapped his knee to brush off the pine needles and set off down the path, leaving Pickett to keep guard. Pickett made himself as comfortable as he could against the birch tree. He had no desire to inspect the body himself. He had lost interest in corpses when he left the homicide unit.

*　　　　*　　　　*

When the police chief returned, he told Pickett he could manage until the Ontario Provincial Police came. Pickett offered to stay, but Caxton shook him off. "You go home. Oh, wait a minute, you don't have a car."

"I'll walk," Pickett said. Caxton obviously wanted to be left alone to get used to what had happened. "I'm getting chilly," Pickett explained. "I'll see you later." Then, for Caxton's sake, he risked insulting him. "Don't try to move it, Lyman. Wait'll they bring in a hook."

Caxton walked up to the tree Pickett had been leaning against and squatted at the base. "Don't you worry about me, old son," he said. "I don't even want to see it anymore, let alone handle it."

CHAPTER 3

Back in the cabin, over more tea, Eliza told him the story.

"When I woke up this morning you could tell that today was going to be the last best day of the year. I turned on the radio and they were playing Mahler, and that did it. I wanted to get out, into the woods."

Pickett wondered if Mahler made you happy or sad. He had heard the name often enough, of course, but it meant nothing. Eliza always talked to him as if he was familiar with her world. Pickett never inquired after her references unless it seemed necessary, preferring not to interrupt the flow just to be clear on every detail. He justified to himself not asking her to stop to unpick every unfamiliar reference by an analogy with his reading practice: when he was reading a book, he didn't stop to look up every new word. Besides, Eliza's inclusion of him in her world was flattering, and well worth a little mystification here and there. It could get embarrassing only if a third person were present, a person as ignorant as he who might ask, after Eliza had gone, who Mahler was. It was a chance he could take. Otherwise, it was exhilarating.

Eliza continued. "I went downstairs and made some coffee and took some up to Dennis. He was awake but he didn't want to get up so I told him if he was feeling amorous, which he was, we could celebrate outside, in the woods with Mahler."

Pickett thought Corning's costume was accounted for now, assembled in a hurry from whatever he'd found on the floor of the bedroom in order to get to the woods before she changed her mind. This was another thing about chatting to Eliza. You could generally count on her in a one-on-one conversation to refer, casually, to some matter that in his experience was usually, if referred to at all, raised only between very close relatives or people who had been friends since high school. He knew that times had changed, and he had wondered at first if she was representative of all lady freelance book editors in their mid-twenties, but he was fairly sure now that either she was an original or she had given him a privileged status. Either way, it made for lively listening. So Mahler, it seemed, made you feel horny.

"It was lovely on that trail, like a blessing, a farewell from the world." She made a Camille-like gesture, enjoying herself for a moment. "The leaves are gorgeous, and enough have come down to make a carpet, especially with the pine needles in the hollows, and the air was patchy—cool and warm alternating like the river water in spring. It was so *physical*. I wanted to go for a swim." Camille, and Pickett, were left behind as Eliza recaptured the excitement she had felt.

"Then you saw the body." Pickett was curious at more than one level.

"Not yet. We lay down to feel the sun in our faces for maybe the last time, you know? And . . . we made love, then Dennis walked down to the gully and shouted, actually called me over, and I went and took a look. Then we came back."

Pickett knew now what she had meant when she had said, "You should have stopped me." Corning should have stopped her from seeing the body. He really did have bad instincts.

"Why did you come to me? Why not go straight into town?"

"Yours is the closest place along this road. Besides, I needed a friend. Dennis . . . Dennis didn't want to report it at all. Let someone else find it, he said. God! I said, we can't just leave it there. Then I remembered you lived here." She turned and examined the cabin. "Are you nearly finished?"

Willis barked at her to be picked up and she lifted the dog awkwardly onto her lap. "Is this what she wants? I don't really like dogs, but she seems very friendly. Will she pee on me or anything?" She stroked Willis inexpertly, catlike, passing her hand down the length of the dog's back. "She's nice. Maybe I'll have a breakthrough."

"The vet called her a tart."

She laughed. "It takes one to know one." She scratched behind Willis's ear with a more spontaneous enthusiasm. "Oh, here they are now." She ran outside, with Pickett following.

Caxton's car turned in at the gate and rolled up to the porch. On the road beyond the fence, an Ontario

Provincial Police patrol car and an ambulance waited, both vehicles with engines running.

"You can go see Dennis now," Caxton said through the car window. He nodded to Pickett, turned the car around, and drove off.

She seemed in no hurry to leave. Pickett guessed the reason. "You feel up to driving?" He lifted Willis from her.

"Would you mind? What about the dog?"

"I'll use my car. We'll take Willis with us. She doesn't mind the back of my station wagon, but she doesn't like strange cars."

"Sensible tart, eh?"

On the way through town, they passed two more OPP cars heading for the scene of the crime. Already small knots of citizens were gathering, asking one another what was going on. Fortunately the tourist season was almost over, or there would have been many more sight-seers. Pickett said, "Can you take it easy the rest of the day?"

She shook her head. "I have to go down to the hall. We've missed too many rehearsals."

"What time does play practice start?"

"Rehearsal, Mel. *Rehearsal*. You make it sound more of a village pageant than it already is. Three o'clock."

Dennis Corning was sitting on the steps of Caxton's house as they drove up. He got in the back of the car and cut short Eliza's inquiries. "The flow of blood to my brain was temporarily halted," he said. "Now I'm fine." He addressed Pickett as if he were a cabdriver. "You know where we're going?"

"Back to my place to get your car. Eliza didn't want to drive."

They continued in silence. At the cabin, Corning said, "I'm very grateful," as if he wasn't. Eliza, flinching at his rudeness, said, "I am, too. 'Bye, Willis."

"Come and see her again," Pickett said.

"I will." She held out her hand, then pulled him forward and kissed him on the cheek. "Thank you for looking after me."

Corning, who had quickly climbed into his own car, said, "For Christ's sake, Eliza, the whole day is shot," and revved his engine.

Eliza responded to this by carefully wiping the nonexistent lipstick from Pickett's cheek, then taking her time walking slowly to the car.

Watching them drive away, Pickett had the feeling that if this were a cartoon, he would be seeing the sides of their car bulge, and steam coming out of the windows to represent what was going on inside.

He had met Eliza earlier in the summer when she had called at the cabin looking to see what she could borrow from him for the first production by the newly formed Larch River Players. One glance had told her that a man building a log cabin does not have an attic full of knickknacks that would dress up a stage, but she had done well from her visit by getting him to agree to come to the community hall to see if there was anything he could do to help out by way of constructing the set. He was happy to take any opportunity to become a part of the community.

When he stopped at the church hall on the following Sunday he learned that he had already been appointed stage carpenter, though there was nothing to be built yet. After that, he often found a reason to drop by on Sunday afternoons to see how things were going. Usually they were going poorly.

The play was based on Goldsmith's *She Stoops to Conquer*, transposed to nineteenth-century Ontario. Two Englishmen, on their way to the wedding of one of them, lose their way in a snowstorm and seek an inn for the night. They are diverted, mischievously, to the house where lives the family of the hero's future bride, a lady he has never met, the marriage having been arranged through a third party. The Englishmen accept the house as an inn, treat the host as a servant, and the host, unaware that he is being mistaken for an innkeeper, gets angrier and angrier at the manners of his guests. Confusion reigns, the mistake is uncovered, and all ends happily.

The playwright, John Dakin, had been forced by ill-health to give up his Toronto teaching job. In search of a less stressful way of life, he had come with his wife, Pat, to Larch River and opened a bed-and-breakfast, hoping that this with his pension would give them a reasonable living, and provide the leisure to pursue his ambition to write. He believed he had a commercial idea in rewriting Goldsmith, and he had formed the Larch River Players with the purpose of seeing where his script needed work. Eliza had gone down to one of the first readings to see if she could help with props, and found herself cast immediately as the heroine, the contracted bride/innkeeper's daughter, who is aware of the mistake but thinks it a great lark and allows her bottom to be pinched to keep the joke going. No other woman under forty was trying out. She also took charge of props. And then, within a very short time, she was the director as well. Pickett got the history of this development from Eliza.

Dakin had begun by directing the play himself, and was also playing the role of host/innkeeper. The trouble began with Pat Dakin, who was originally cast as the hostess, refusing to take his direction. He had tried to curb her movements a little, pointing out that her natural carriage was fine, there was no need to stride about like a male ballet dancer just because she was on stage. Feeling herself humiliated in front of the other actors, she flew into a temper and quit, and had to be replaced by the wife of the United Church minister, who took the part on condition the word *fart* was taken out of the script. But the problems mounted as the playwright/director made unreasonable demands on his amateur cast, and the actors got together one Friday night in the hardware store and decided that they would not carry on if he stayed as director.

When the spokesperson put it to him, Dakin asked them rhetorically who else could do the job and was told they wanted Eliza to try; when she arrived, they told her what they had decided. "I'd seen this coming, and I had no intention of saying yes. I mean, all I wanted to do in the first place was show my willingness to get involved a little, if we were going to live here, but in the end, they said that it was either me in charge or no play. There wasn't anyone else."

"Did you know anything about directing?" Pickett asked.

"Not a thing, but I found a book which gave me some vocabulary, like what 'stage left' and 'stage right' mean. That keeps me slightly ahead of the actors. So far, we've managed." She laughed. "The fact is, they love me and I love them, and I'm having a ball."

The police came back just as Pickett was thinking of quitting work for the day. The cars pulled up first beside the little house trailer he had lived in while he was building the cabin, then rolled forward to where he was cementing rocks into place for the first corner foundation of the platform he wanted to build in front of the porch. He was eager to get the platform done before winter, because with a decent deck out front he would be able to keep a supply of wood handy, and step outside for a log without breaking his ankle on a snow-covered rock. His whole building program had proceeded on such a system of seasonal priorities.

Pickett put down his trowel and waited for Caxton and the two OPP officers to approach. He recognized them both for what they were. The younger of them, a slim, fair-haired man of about thirty, was unmistakable. The suit, the tie, the neat haircut and even neater mustache all proclaimed him a recently mustered plainclothes policeman. The other, older, perhaps forty-five, might have passed for a construction foreman dressed to see his lawyer: a bald head over a bushy mustache, hands that seemed too big even for the thick body, the dressy tie that created a culture clash with the check bush shirt, gray tweed jacket, and heavy boots. Judging by his clothes, he was the one who had gone down into the crevasse.

Caxton made to introduce them but the older policeman was already shaking Pickett's hand. "I wondered if there could be two of you," he said.

"Abraham Wilkie. Or his dad."

"Fuck you, Mel Pickett. My dad's an old fart, like you."

"You guys know each other, I guess," Caxton said.

Pickett removed his hand from Wilkie's clamp. "He used to work under me," he explained to Caxton. "I used to wipe his nose for him." He started to lead the way up the steps, then turned back. "Let's stay outside." He pointed to the wooden table and chairs assembled in the shade of a large birch tree. "I'll make some coffee."

Wilkie gave up trying to think of an insult in exchange for Pickett's, and the three men sat down while Pickett disappeared into the house. When he returned with cups, cream, sugar, and a *cafetière* of coffee, Wilkie saw his opportunity. "No croissants?" he asked.

Pickett said, "I guess you're not used to anything like this in Sweetwater, eh? But I do have an old enamel jug I picked up in a barn sale. I keep it under the bed to piss in to save going outside in cold weather. I could boil up a handful of coffee grounds in that, open a can of Carnation milk if that'd make you feel more at home."

"Doughnuts would be nice."

Pickett pressed down the plunger and poured out the coffee. "So what did you find?" he asked.

But Wilkie had a lot he wanted to know first. "How long you been up here, Mel?"

"This is my third year."

"Who built your cabin?"

"He did," Caxton said. "By himself." Caxton's interjection was quick and dismissive. Wilkie's rediscovery of Pickett had put him in a larky mood but Caxton could not relax with this banter. The body they had found had drained all the cheeriness from his face.

Wilkie stood up to take a good look at the cabin. "I'm impressed. Was it in a kit?"

"It's a hundred-year-old cabin he reassembled by himself." Again Caxton spoke impatiently, wanting the topic disposed of.

Wilkie ignored him. "I really am impressed. Can I have a look around?"

They waited while he disappeared inside. Caxton took the chance to introduce Pickett to the younger policeman, who had been waiting to be noticed. "Brendan Copps," he said. Copps thrust out his hand as soon as Caxton began the introduction.

Wilkie called out from the door of the cabin, "You going to keep a pig, Mel? Few chickens?"

"Not inside," Pickett said. "Our family hasn't done that since my great-grandfather's day. Maybe I should, though. What's it like? You remember?"

Wilkie grinned.

"So," Caxton said loudly, signaling that it was time to get the meeting underway.

Wilkie returned and took his seat, turning to Pickett. "I heard your name from Lyman here. An old cop, someone said, turning into a hermit. I had to see."

"He didn't tell me he knew you," Caxton said. "I couldn't figure out why we were bothering you." He looked around at the group as if to see who was in charge. "You guys need me? I'd like to get over to see Betty."

Wilkie held up a hand to retain Caxton, nodding to show he had heard the request. He hitched his chair close to the table. "I think we've got a homicide," he said. "At the very least, leaving the scene of an accident."

Several seconds of silence followed this. Pickett looked at Caxton.

"Was it in bad shape?" Pickett asked.

Wilkie said, "He's been there a couple of days, I'd say. Some kind of animals found him, you know that. Hard to recognize, but his wallet was still there, and his watch." He reached into his pocket and drew out a wristwatch and a wallet wrapped in a bandanna. He pulled the edge of the scarf and let the wallet unwrap itself on the table. "Lyman could identify him."

Caxton said, "It's Timmy Marlow, Betty's brother. I should have recognized the jacket when we were first up there."

Pickett, remembering Caxton's reaction to the body, remembering thinking that Caxton was being squeamish, now thought, You probably did. You just didn't know how you should react. Did you know Marlow hadn't been around this weekend? Had Betty been worrying about him?

When the silence had endured long enough, Pickett said, "You taking it to Sweetwater?"

"I called forensic first. That place he's in is like a stone coffin. I got down there with a rope but there's no way we could bring him out without our equipment. Besides, they may find something when they're lifting him out that I wouldn't notice." He met Pickett's glance blandly, knowing that Pickett would realize that he was just passing on an unpleasant job.

"Didn't Betty miss him?" Pickett asked Caxton.

"She didn't say anything to me this morning," Caxton said.

"Does she know yet?"

Caxton shook his head. "Christ, Mel, she doted on him. I'm not looking forward to telling her. She isn't feeling too good already. She thought she was getting flu yesterday."

Copps, the younger OPP officer, shifted restlessly. Wilkie turned to him suddenly. "Brendan, why don't you go back with the chief here? See if there are any messages on his fax for us. Start putting together the statements and our preliminary report. Okay? And Lyman, don't go far away, eh? I have to ask Mrs. Cullen a few questions. I'd like you there."

"You just going to sit here and shoot the shit for a couple of hours?" Copps asked. The tone was almost insulting.

Wilkie said, "I might. This guy and me go back a long way. I'd like to hear about this cabin. When you come back, if we're still talking, wait in the road. Okay?" He stared at Copps until the policeman stood up. Caxton still looked a little lost, as if he wanted to stay.

"You can leave us alone, Lyman," Pickett said. "We haven't seen each other for a while. Got to catch up. Here, Willis." He picked the dog up and waited for the car to disappear down the road.

CHAPTER 4

When the cars left, Pickett said, "What's the problem with your buddy?"

"He's restless, you know? Wants to arrest somebody."

Pickett laughed. "The guy he wants left town two days ago, tell him. There's no hurry. I'll get us a beer."

"Not for me, Mel. I have to interview the citizens."

"More coffee, then?"

Wilkie nodded. He picked up a book on bird-watching and leafed through it, grinning. "You into this now?" he asked.

Pickett decided not to favor him with the truth. When he began building his cabin, it had not occurred to him that he might seem eccentric—he just wanted to build a cabin—but it soon became clear that he had better have a cover story, so he bought three books on birds and a pair of binoculars, and Larch River accepted him as an old widower who wanted a place to watch birds in peace. Odd, of course, but just comprehensible. Pickett did learn to identify three or four of the more obvious birds, but apart from cardinals and blue jays, he found them uninteresting. Now, to Wilkie, he said, "A whole new world has opened up to me, Wilkie, old son. Saw a yellow-bellied nit-picker this morning. They're very rare in these parts."

Wilkie, though, smelled a rat, and protected himself from being sucked in. "It's the red-assed curry-bird that you want to watch out for," he said. "Really make your name, seeing one of them would."

While Pickett made coffee, Wilkie walked around the cabin, surveying the grounds. When he returned he asked, "What do you use the trailer for? Guests?"

"I had to have somewhere to stay while I got this place up. I tried the bed-and-breakfast route. Once was enough."

"What was the problem? No croissants for breakfast? We're not used to your big-city ways in these parts."

"Matter of fact there were croissants. One, anyway. And grapes, and an apple all cut up in artistic slices. Pretty dishes and napkins, too. The croissant, though, was still frozen in the middle. Afterward I went into town for something to eat. I decided that if I was going to spend any time here I'd better make some serious arrangements for eating and sleeping, so I bought the trailer."

"You really like it here?"

"I haven't had time to find out; I've been too busy building. I never planned to live here. I just wanted to see if I could build a log cabin like they used to."

"And that's what you did. Just like that. A real pioneer."

"Nearly. They didn't have chain saws, though."

"How long has it taken you?"

"Two years, more or less. I didn't know a thing about it, and now I know, I wouldn't do it again."

"That's true of anything I've ever built. Now . . ."

"To start with I had no idea that it would be hard to find trees, you know. The pioneers had first-growth cedar to work with, but that's all gone. Nobody in Toronto told me. But I found a guy who owned a tree plantation and he had what I wanted. I *did* cut it myself, and he arranged to have it hauled here. Then I peeled the logs, ready for the next spring."

"Were they dry enough to use then?"

"I never got a chance to find out. Some bastard with a chain saw and a truck stole the lot in the winter." Wilkie would hear the story eventually. Might as well hear it from Pickett now.

Wilkie threw back his head, roaring with glee. "Then what'd you do?"

"There was a bright side. People around here all heard about it, and when they stopped laughing they felt sorry for me, offered to help out, some of them. Nobody actually said he'd help me cut down some more trees but they would probably have joined in at a barn-raising kind of thing. Anyway, one of them heard of a guy who knew of another guy near Bancroft who owned a gas station and had to take down an old log cabin to expand his business. So I made him an offer and he numbered all the logs as he dismantled the cabin. I got a trucker to bring them up here. Then one of my new friends came up with a cousin with an A-frame on the back of a one-ton truck, and between me, him, his cousin, and the A-frame we got it up in three days."

"It *was* kind of a kit, then?"

Pickett understood that Wilkie wasn't jeering, just trying to get a fix on how much he should admire

Pickett's achievement. It sounded like jeering, though. Pickett was very proud of his cabin, but he tried not to be a bore about the building of it. Wilkie, though, would have to be told. "I didn't start with a broadax and a stand of virgin cedar, no," he said. "But I learned a lot, even so. Let me show you how this place was put together."

Wilkie started to say something, looking at his watch, but Pickett ignored him. He cleared his throat. "For example, this cabin is twenty-five feet by fifteen. Know why?"

Wilkie gave a quick shake of his head, a polite little shake between nods. Already his eyes had started to glaze.

"Because they built them out of fifty-foot trees."

Wilkie tried to step farther back, to make breaking-off signs.

Pickett said, "They cut the trees in half, see, to get the twenty-five-footers. Then the top half, the other twenty-five-footers, they cut into two pieces, one fifteen, one ten. You follow? Now they used the fifteen-footers along the sides, and the ten-foot pieces they split into rails to line the walls with. See what I mean? Come over here. See?"

"I see, yeah, I see . . ."

"Now come over here." Pickett walked to the window. "See the way this window is framed? Two-by-ten-inch lumber attached to the logs with *dowelling*. See? Take a look, go ahead. There's one dowel, there's another."

Wilkie said, "Mel . . ."

"Now," Pickett continued. "You must have wondered, too, why the roof doesn't overhang the walls. Right? Well, that's so it won't collapse under the weight of snow. They notched the roof right into the walls, see? Tell you something else," he added as Wilkie opened his mouth. "You ever heard the expression 'putting on side'?"

Wilkie shook his head.

"Man I hired to do the plastering told me about that. Said some of the wives of the early pioneers used to get their husbands to pretty up the outside of the cabins by putting on siding. Get it? Now . . ."

"Mel, I have to get back to Sweetwater today . . ."

"Right you are, old son. There *is* a lot more to tell, though, if you're ever interested. You should build one yourself. I'll show you how."

Wilkie said, "I did think of it once. I won't now, though. Are you going to live here?"

"I never planned to, but I'm starting to feel at home here. I've still got to civilize it. Put in a shower. Bring it into the twentieth century. I plan to spend weekends in the cabin, probably until the end of January. Then I'll go to Florida for a couple of weeks, then spend a week or so in Toronto, then another couple of weeks in England, and then, if there's still no sign of spring, I'll go back to Florida to wait. What's *your* life like?"

Wilkie took a long pull of his coffee and walked to the window. "I miss Toronto," he said finally, his voice indicating that he was no longer bantering. "I miss the city. Working in Sweetwater is like being in the Mounties. When I was off-duty in Toronto I was *really* off-duty, but in Sweetwater everyone knows I'm a cop. And they shift us around, too. My wife hates that. If I get posted to northwest Ontario, I think she'll take off." He stopped, looking slightly ashamed of his confession. "And yet you're totally happy up here in Rainbow County."

"I'm not a cop anymore and I told you, I don't live here. Besides, this isn't too rugged. I did a lot of looking before I picked this place. I decided that three hours was the maximum I wanted to drive. More than that, you have to stop for coffee."

"Who else lives here in the winter?"

"The core population, which is bigger than you'd think. This place doesn't rely as much on the tourists as some of the others around here. Those boarded-up food places on the highway make it look as if the whole town's closed up, but it isn't."

"What the hell do people here *do* in the winter?" The question was rhetorical. Wilkie sighed and went back to work. "You know this guy Caxton?"

"He came out to check on me a couple of times when I was first building the place. He found out I was on the force—I hadn't retired yet—so that made us buddies as far as he was concerned. He's never been a regular cop, though. He was in the Lands and Forests Department once, some kind of fire ranger or warden, then he owned a marina near Peterborough, which went belly-up, and then he came here. He likes the fishing and the hunting, and I think he had some idea of opening another business, a bait shop or some such. He worked for one or two of the people here for a while, then the town gave him a job. He suits this place. He likes being the police chief, and he puts in a lot of extra time he doesn't get paid for."

"Seems like a bit of a Boy Scout," Wilkie said.

"Conscientious, you mean?" He knew exactly what Wilkie meant, but he was slightly offended by Wilkie's assumption that Pickett was as much of an outsider as he was. For all Wilkie knew, Pickett and Caxton were buddies.

Wilkie said, "I figured he sees himself kind of like—who was that guy who played small-town cops?—Andy Griffith."

"He does his job, and they like him well enough, so it's his for life. I told you, he's conscientious, and he makes sure he knows what's happening around town. I like the guy. I know what you mean, sure. He enjoys having his picture taken with his hat on, but he doesn't think he's John Wayne and there's a whole other side to him. He makes me feel like a city boy sometimes. A dumb one."

Wilkie waited for more.

"He knows about animals, stuff like that. Just a small for instance, he's the only one who can get Willis to sit still. I don't know what he does, maybe he's got some secret signal, but he just says 'sit' and Willis sits. Willis won't do it for me. I'm impressed. Tell you the truth, I sometimes think he's kind of like a big animal himself, like a bear or something. Other times, okay, I agree, he looks like he's trying to imitate Andy Hardy. Was that his name?"

"Griffith. Caxton would know the area, then."

"Oh, sure. And I would think he knows just about everyone around here."

Wilkie looked at his watch again. "This guy Marlow. Did you know him? He was Caxton's girlfriend's brother, right?"

"I knew him to see. Bit of a dude. Sideburns. Little curly beard."

"He's clean-shaven now. Caxton and this woman live together? Or just go around for company?"

"You see them around at barbecues, picnics, stuff like that. If you're asking me if they sleep together, I don't know, but my assumption would be yes. But they don't live together."

"I just want to know if we should keep an eye on him. He could be a lot of help. Being a local, he might have some idea of who would kill Marlow. But if he's real close to Marlow's sister, then he might get some idea of avenging his woman, something like that. He could be very useful, but I don't want him conducting his own investigation on the side, know what I mean?"

"Tell him. Tell him the procedure when one of us has a personal stake in a case. I think he'll keep his distance. But, like you said, he could be a lot of help to you, too."

"Did he get along with Marlow okay?"

Pickett had known this was coming, known that Wilkie was making his list already. "You'll have to ask someone else that. Someone who knows them better. He a suspect?"

Wilkie laughed. "You know how it is, Mel. *You're* a suspect. So as far as you know, Caxton and this guy were pals?"

The truth was so far from this that Pickett would have to have been blind and deaf not to get some inkling

49

of it; he saw no point in continuing to dodge. "I don't know Caxton well, but I'm pretty sure he didn't like Marlow at all. That's what I've heard. But when he saw whose body it was, I think he might have recognized him and foreseen a lot of misery for himself. He looked to me like he wished he was in Florida right then."

"That's helpful. What about Marlow?"

"If I racked my brains I could probably come up with something I'd heard that accounts for the fact that my impression is that he wasn't very popular. Maybe threw his weight around. Which would mean that Caxton had some problems, but I'm not aware of any confrontations between them. Now you have everything I know."

"Now we have to 'search the area,' " Wilkie said. "Christ. You know anything about that part of the bush?"

"I told you, take Caxton with you. What would you hope to find?"

"Nothing. If someone local killed him, the guy's been sitting at home all weekend, scared to poke his nose out. But just in case he's holed up in one of the cottages still, we have to look the area over." Wilkie stood up and put his cup on the table. "Good to talk to you, Mel. I'll let you know how it goes."

"You'll come by and pick my brains, you mean?"

Wilkie laughed. "Yeah, pick your brains about the locals, if this doesn't get cleaned up quick. Maybe just come by for a chat. I'll tell Dad I ran into you. Bird-watching."

In Caxton's office, Brendan Copps said, "I guess we should let his sister know."

"I'll do that," Caxton said. He could not put it off any longer. The news would reach the bakery soon enough, and he should be the one who brought it.

"You know her pretty well?"

"I've lived here for ten goddamn years. There's only one baker in the town."

Copps looked up, surprised at the violence of Caxton's tone. "Did I say something wrong?"

Caxton waved the question away and got to his feet.

Copps continued. "Town this size, you must have known her brother pretty good."

"All I wanted to. I'll go over there now," he said. "Your boss will know where to find you. The people you sent for are coming to the office here, right?"

"I imagine." The policeman slumped back in his chair.

"You want a beer?" Caxton asked.

The OPP man shook his head. "My boss might disapprove." He pulled himself out of his chair. "I'd better go get him."

CHAPTER 5

Half an hour later Wilkie appeared on Caxton's porch and asked him to take them to interview Betty.

"I've already let her know," Caxton said. "She should be all right by now."

"Why didn't you wait for me?"

"Because she's a friend of mine. And because I didn't want someone phoning her. The whole town knows by now."

Wilkie blinked and frowned. "I guess the possibility that she shot her brother is remote, all right. But don't help us out too much, okay? It's our investigation now."

"That it is. And she's my girlfriend. Let's go over there."

"Can we walk?"

"It's three blocks." He nodded at the window. "You can see the sign on the other side, past the cold storage warehouse."

"Let's walk, then. You can fill me in on the way over."

Caxton had anticipated all of Wilkie's questions. "I couldn't stand the guy," he said finally, telling Wilkie what he was bound to find out, anyway. "For one thing, he's the reason me and Betty aren't married. Here we are now." They paused outside the bakery, Wilkie waiting for more. Caxton continued, "Marlow had a couple of arrests in Sweetwater for drunk driving and one for assault. Around here, he liked to hang out with the dregs, like Siggy Siggurdson and Joe McBain. There's a table of them in the beer parlor by the motel most nights. A day was coming when I would have had to arrest him for something, sure as eggs, or resign. Even now, some people around here figure I've been protecting him because of Betty. For me he was awkward as hell and I wished he'd go away. The reason Betty wouldn't marry me was because she figured Timmy was liable to become too big an embarrassment for me. We'd just sorted that out, and then he gets himself killed and I'm out again. This time the reason he was killed, she thinks, might be embarrassing for the chief of police. Now you know it all. Can we get this over with?"

Wilkie knocked at the door.

Betty Cullen was a small, pretty woman in her mid-forties, plump with a full bosom and thick brown curly hair cut close to her head. She led them through the shop and the bakery behind, into the back room. Although it was Sunday she closed off the doors as they passed through them, as if to keep the customers from hearing anything.

She had had only half an hour to digest the news, and she was obviously under considerable strain, but she answered all Wilkie's questions without hesitation.

"When did you see your brother last?" he began.

"On Friday. Friday afternoon."

"Did you know of his plans for the weekend?"

"He told me he was going to Toronto. I assumed to see some woman he had there."

"Why? Why did you assume that?"

"He was a womanizer." There was no stress on the word. She might have been calling him a music-lover. Only the choice of word showed her attitude.

"Where did he stay?"

"Like, live? Here. He lived here." She pointed upstairs.

"Could you show me his room?" He turned to Caxton. "Tell Copps to come over, would you?"

She led the way upstairs and to the front of the house, and opened a door onto a small room with a single bed, a pine bureau, and an old wardrobe. The wide floorboards had been sanded recently and varnished, and were partially covered with braided cotton rugs. The room was clean, the bed was made, and there were no clothes in sight.

"Won't be hard to check this out," Wilkie said. "He was a tidy guy."

"*I'm* tidy. He was my brother. I looked after him."

"You've been in here since he left on Friday?"

"I cleaned it."

"Did you take anything away?"

"His dirty laundry."

"Where is that now?"

"In the dryer."

They were interrupted by the arrival of Copps. Wilkie said, "We won't need you for a while, Mrs. Cullen. Or you, Lyman."

When the others had retreated downstairs, Wilkie told Copps what to look for. "It's routine," he said. "Covering our ass, if you like. Look around, go through any papers, letters, stuff like that. Find anything that'll tell us who he meets in Toronto, or who he was meeting here. Find anything he might have been hiding from his sister."

Back in the sitting room, Wilkie said, "Who were your brother's friends, Mrs. Cullen? Could you give me a list?"

She shook her head. "I couldn't. Try the beer parlor, eh, Lyman? I never wanted to know who the women were."

"I'll give you a list of his cronies afterward," Caxton volunteered.

Wilkie nodded and stood up.

Caxton said, "You want me to stay, Betty? I could come right back . . ."

"Not now, Lyman," she said. "No. I need to be by myself. Leave me alone." She looked around abruptly. "All of you. Leave me *alone*." She opened the door, urging them out.

Wilkie said, "Officer Copps will be through upstairs shortly."

She absorbed this silently, holding the door open, her head down, waiting for them to go.

Out on the street, Wilkie said to Caxton, "She doesn't know anything about how he spent his time, does she? She isn't going to be much help."

Caxton said nothing.

"I suppose if she could help us find who killed little Timmy, she would. Wouldn't you think? Could you bring her in tomorrow to identify him?"

"Jesus Christ, couldn't I do that? The guy's been dead a couple of days. He's not pretty."

"I know, but I need a next-of-kin ID. Now let's take a look at those cottages. What's the best way to do that?"

"We'll do it from the river. I'll get my boat from Chester's marina."

Wilkie looked at his watch. "I'd better go talk to the pair who found the body, first. You have an address?"

Caxton led them into his office and wrote out Dennis Corning's address, adding directions.

Wilkie said, "I'll call you when I'm done."

When Wilkie had gone, Pickett lay down for a twenty-minute nap, put a collar on Willis, then changed his mind and left the dog to guard the house while he went to town. He had long ago given up trying to get Willis to behave in public without a leash, and even on a leash Willis spent most of his time trying to trip Pickett.

He tried to get the heavy work done in the mornings now, and putter for the rest of the day: a drive to town to pick up the newspaper and whatever groceries and building supplies he needed, a chat with whoever looked glad to see him, and then home for his chief pleasure, an hour's read. He read a lot and tried everything. He had recently come across Winston Graham and become engrossed, and then happy that the Poldarks would last him for years. That hour was his only reading time. When he retired, he had thought he would read in the evenings, but he simply wasn't alert enough, so he tinkered with little jobs, like sharpening his chain saw, or listened to the radio if he could find a baseball game or someone talking. So far he had resisted bringing a television set up to the cabin, but in the battle to avoid going to bed earlier and earlier, and therefore being awake in the too small hours, he had wondered lately if a television might be the answer.

When Pickett first began to try to get to know the members of the community who might be useful to him, he soon learned that many of the jobs he would need help with would require the services of people who did not necessarily advertise their skills. The well digger had a sign outside his house, as did the electrician and the ladies' hairdresser, but for most other jobs you had to know where to find the man. In Sweetwater, for example, five miles away, there was a licensed plumber who would send a man to a house in Larch River for forty-five dollars an hour (ninety on Sundays), but the man he would send actually lived in Larch River and he moonlighted for twenty-five an hour if he knew you. You could find someone locally to do almost anything, from building a fireplace to felling a tree, but you had to know where to look. (The postmistress was his best source of information. In exchange he satisfied her curiosity about himself.) For hauling and laboring jobs, there were plenty of people who owned pickup trucks and who were happy to earn a few dollars on a Saturday afternoon. But you had to know and be known, and Pickett had made a point of buying everything in town as far as possible, including gas, and he ate, by design at first and then by inclination, in the coffee shop by the service station.

He pulled into one of the spaces beside the motel, knowing that he ought to be talking to Lyman Caxton, keeping him company, but putting it off for a while. He walked into the little café, a separate building beside the gas pumps, and Charlotte Mercer waited for him to choose a stool, then put his coffee in front of him. There was only one other customer, a traveler stopped for gas, and Pickett sipped his coffee and rearranged the contents of his wallet until the man left and Charlotte had poured herself a glass of water and sat down next to him, holding the cloth she had been using to wipe the counter. She had a round face with small gray eyes that disappeared when she smiled. Her nose was turned up and too small for her face, and it seemed alive, constantly twitching, or dilating, or wrinkling, or all at once. Pickett thought at first that she was responding to a temporary irritant but now he was used to the idea that Charlotte just liked to exercise her nose. The rest of her was solid without being fat, not very much waist and slightly chunky legs. She wore a white nylon uniform in the café, slightly too tight around the bottom, and running shoes.

"You heard?" Pickett asked.

"Four people in already to tell me. Maybe there's someone in town who hasn't heard, but I doubt it."

"You knew him well?"

"He brought the bread around. I liked him better when he first came here, six, seven years ago. He kept pretty much to himself then. Last couple of years he's been a bit more—active. He seemed to think he was too good for Larch River, went around like the city boy among a bunch of farmers. And there are other stories." She made a face and sipped some water, waiting.

"Like what?"

"Two or three people stopped buying their bread because of him. He kept a Mickey of rye in the glove compartment of the truck. People smelled it on him in the morning. It didn't bother me. Betty needs the business, and my customers like her bread."

"That all? Just a few swigs on the job?"

"He was late sometimes. Usually on the days I was running low. Who do they think did it?"

Pickett instinctively tried to dampen speculation. "They haven't started to find out yet. Could have been an accident."

She considered her next comment. "He was a skirt-chaser, I heard."

"Any particular skirt?"

"I heard he wasn't particular." She raised her head and smiled at the row of boxes of Kellogg's Corn Flakes behind the counter. "I think that's what made him late sometimes."

Pickett grinned. "Did he ever make a pass at you?"

She laughed. "You think I'm too old? For him?"

"No way."

"He gave me a big smacker one day when there was no one around, and said Merry Christmas. That count?"

"That all?"

"It was October."

"What did you do?"

"I burned his toast. Nothing. That was the best offer I'd had in years." She laughed. "I didn't mind, except he'd had a snort." She looked at the clock and slid off the stool. "You coming for supper?"

She ran the tiny restaurant as if it were her own kitchen, cooking specials of meat loaf or stuffed roast pork every day for the regulars, and baking her own butter tarts and muffins. Once Pickett had discovered the coffee shop, he was in there more often than a man who had cooked for himself for years needed to be, even for political reasons. But Charlotte closed early on Sundays because she liked to cook her Sunday supper at home and because there was hardly any business. Then one Saturday, they got talking, and Charlotte invited him up to her house for supper on Sunday and that had become a regular thing.

"What time?" he asked.

"We'll eat about seven. I've got a chicken. A good one. Farmer from Sweetwater brings them around on Saturdays. Fresh killed, they are. I asked him if they were free range like they have in the city; he said no, but they get out a lot."

Pickett nodded, hardly listening. "Where did Marlow come from? Where did he live before he came here?"

"I thought that was cute," she said, making a face. "Why are you so interested in Marlow? He just appeared. Betty said she sent for him to help her out, but I never thought she needed any help. I reckon he was out of work before." She thought it over. "Somewhere out west, I think. I know Betty was born in Manitoba."

"How long's she been here?"

"Fifteen years, easy. Her husband came here to open the bakery. He set it up, then he died. Cancer, I think. And she just carried on."

"How old is she?"

"Forty-five, anyway. There was a big gap between her and Timmy. I guess that's why she felt so protective of her little brother. He was her only family."

The door *pinged* and a man came in, another stranger off the highway. She touched the back of Pickett's hand and moved to serve the customer. Pickett put a dollar on the counter and left while Charlotte was taking the man's order.

As he drove along Queen Street to Caxton's house, he was conscious of being looked at, already connected by the rumors to the body on the trail, but none of the people he passed knew him well enough to stop him and ask questions. He was surprised to catch the police chief on a ladder, once more putting on his storm windows as if nothing had happened; it looked like Caxton was trying to keep his distance from the investigation by finding any kind of thing to do to stay busy.

Caxton waved to Pickett as he approached. "Get yourself a beer from the house. Bring one out for me. Great day, huh? " He looked down at Pickett. "Or it was."

"I'll come back," Pickett said. "When you've finished your windows."

"No, no. Stop a minute. I can do this later." Caxton came down the ladder and rolled up his hose. He coiled it onto the reel attached to the wall of the house.

"Mebbe pick up the windows, too," Pickett suggested, looking at the windows spread out on the grass, then up at the brittle-looking branches of an old apple tree already shuddering in the freshening wind.

Together the two men stacked the storm windows against the house.

"I think I've reached the turning point," Caxton said. "Next spring I'm going to get those aluminum storms and screens you don't have to screw around with. I've always kinda liked this job, you know? Sunny day, spread the windows out, hose 'em down, wipe 'em off with a paper towel. Even going up the ladder with them wasn't bad. And when you finish, when you've got the windows on and the screens stacked in the basement, it's a lot quieter indoors. It's fall; you can light a little fire, even if you don't need it yet, put the fishing gear away, get out your curling sweater. You know? But this year, tell the truth, for the first time, it's a pain in the ass." He pointed to the big storm windows. "Those suckers are *heavy* when you're on the top of a ladder. I'm too *old*, Mel. Too goddamn *old*. Not enough energy left to put up storm windows *and* have some left over." Then, suddenly, he stopped trying to act normal. "And next year I'll remember what we found today and know it's time to put up the windows. Betty's pretty upset," he concluded.

They went inside and Caxton sat at his tidy desk, holding a bottle of beer, looking out the window down the road as if waiting for something to happen. In a few minutes he moved twice from the desk to an armchair and back again.

"Maybe you should be with her," Pickett said.

"She doesn't want anybody around. Not me, not anybody."

Pickett did not know Caxton well enough to respond to this. "Did Wilkie's crew find anything more?" he asked.

"He was shot, they know that. Probably with a small handgun, something like mine."

"Did they find the gun?"

"Not yet."

"So it wasn't suicide."

"I guess we all know what it was, eh?"

"Nothing else?"

"Not connected to him."

"Any ideas?"

"Not my investigation, is it? Thank Christ. Can you see me questioning Betty? I've told those guys what I know. They can take it from there." He got up and moved to the window, talking sideways and over his shoulder.

"Will Betty be able to run the bakery by herself?"

"Oh, sure. He wasn't much use. When he wanted to work he had a strong back, but half the time he was dogging it, down in the beer parlor, over to Jensen's, stuff like that. She couldn't rely on him. Didn't stop her defending the bastard, though. She thought he was a good boy in bad company, thought he'd straighten around any day." Caxton stopped moving, looked at Pickett, and licked his lips. "He was a thirty-year-old bum and a useless tit, and worse. I know he was taking money out of the till all the time. Betty wouldn't admit it. I saw the son of a bitch fill his wallet once when I was coming in through the back of the bakery. When I told her, she said she knew, she'd told him to." Caxton's tone was savage.

"He's dead now, Lyman," Pickett reminded him. "Somebody killed him. Would anybody he hangs around with go that far?"

"He's been in a couple of fights. Used to drink with some guys from Dumpey's Mill, and anyone else who was around. He put a guy in the hospital once, in a fight in Sweetwater, but the guy wouldn't lay a charge."

"There's a few suspects, then."

"When they get a better idea of when he was killed, they'll check them out. If it was one of them, I guess they'll find him."

"Any other possibilities?"

Caxton relaxed slightly, the talk helping. "I'm wondering if it could've been connected with the stolen stuff in those cottages along the river."

CHAPTER 6

Caxton was talking about an outbreak of theft and vandalism that had occurred among the cottages along the shore. The previous spring, owners arriving to open up their cottages on the Victoria Day weekend, the traditional cottage-opening weekend at the end of May, had found they had all been broken into. Any liquor they had left was gone, though not much else, and the beds had been used, condoms left behind; in one cottage was a calling card in the form of a turd in the middle of the floor.

The signs did not add up to a real thief, but—and here the turd was significant, according to one of the OPP—to a gesture of contempt from Indians who were trying to reclaim the land as their own. He had brought this theory with him from his last posting near Parry Sound, but, as the locals pointed out, it didn't make much sense in Larch River because the nearest Indian band was thirty miles away. The actual damage was negligible, and there was not much to be done about it, anyway. The OPP cruised along the river attaching little labels to the cottages, assuring the owners that the area was being patrolled, but as the locals remarked, you would have to be drunk, stone deaf, and crippled not to hear them coming and have all the time in the world to disappear in the bush before they tied up at the dock. Some of the owners demanded a response from the police, and for these Caxton filled out a form; others, more philosophically, left their doors unlocked so that intruders would not have to break them down, and took their liquor home with them but left behind a couple of bottles of beer to avoid irritating the callers.

The incidents had continued sporadically all summer. Whoever was doing it seemed to know which cottages were uninhabited during the week. Two of the cottages were owned by Larch River residents; the others, by summer visitors. The cottages of the two locals were never violated, so it seemed clear that the vandals were local people. Caxton had suggested to the OPP that occasional aerial reconnaissance might help—the police had been lucky once in solving a case of theft of a canoe by picking out the boat's hiding place from the air. And then one night a high school student had had a seizure after he had made love to his girlfriend in one of the cottages, and she had had to go for help and explain the circumstances in case it was the sex that had triggered his fit. After that it was agreed that Larch River's own teenagers were probably to blame for all the incidents. Caxton got a list from the boy who had had the fit and visited the teenagers in their homes. After that, no more condoms were found, but the thefts continued.

There were levels of knowledge involved in using the land along the river. In general the cottage owners knew only the bit of land they owned, to a depth of about fifty yards behind them. They came and went by boat, ignoring the bush in the back. Some of the Larch River locals, chiefly the hunters, knew the trail that Marlow's body had been found on, but only one or two people were familiar with the whole area.

Pickett said, "You don't think some kid shot him?"

"What I think is that it wasn't always kids who stole the stuff from the cottages. We just blamed them so we could forget about it."

"Do you know which cottages were occupied?"

"That OPP guy is planning to take a poke around." Caxton looked at his watch. "He asked me to go up with them. I don't think there are any cottagers up there now, but if there are, someone could've heard a shot, then they might get an idea as to the time and start to pin everyone down. Trouble is, you spend half an hour on the river at this time of year and you'll hear shooting, someone doing a little target practice waiting for the hunting season to open. There's a target on a tree up behind the Broda cottage." The last of his edginess faded as he began to speculate.

"Maybe someone like that hit Marlow by mistake."

Caxton looked hopeful. "You don't go hunting with a handgun, Mel, but it might turn out to be an accident. What it could be is one of the cottagers from the city looking to scare off what they thought was an animal, and killing Marlow."

Pickett looked skeptical. "Even people from Toronto don't fire off guns at noises in the bush. Not adults."

Caxton continued, "Fact is, lately someone's started to really steal stuff. The thieving's getting serious, you might say—fishing tackle, radios, even a generator from the Schultzes' place."

Pickett nodded. "That's more than kids looking for a place to screw."

"That's what I'm saying. Maybe Timmy did a little stealing himself. Then we're back to thinking someone took a shot at him when he was where he shouldn't be and didn't miss. Maybe one of the American owners. It's legal in the States, you know. If a guy breaks into your house you can blow him away. If you do that here, you have to be sure to kill him, otherwise he'll sue you for assault. You could wind up supporting him for life."

Pickett nodded at the familiar story, which Caxton had got from a Mountie, who might have been joking. "The OPP know all the possibilities?"

"Sure. They're nearly as smart as you are, Mel." He laughed briefly, then suddenly brought his hand down hard on the desk. "Son of a bitch. I knew that bastard would screw up me and Betty in the end. Never a day went by without I wondered if I would have to arrest him for something, and Betty wouldn't understand why I had to."

It made no sense, except that it made sense of why Caxton had been so agitated when Pickett arrived. Pickett would not have been surprised to learn that Marlow had taken advantage of the relationship to claim a little immunity in minor matters, drunkenness and speeding, for example. But now, as far as he could see, the problem of Timmy Marlow had solved itself. Caxton and Betty could grieve, a little hypocritically in Caxton's case, then pursue a much easier relationship. "Why would she blame you?" he asked, more or less rhetorically.

"She's afraid of what may come out." Caxton gestured vaguely to cover the unknown. "So am I." Then he turned away abruptly and reached for his holster. "She thinks he may have been part of the cottage problem, too, I guess. Something like that." Caxton was cutting the conversation off. He opened the drawer for his gun, buckling it into the holster, stuffing change and a ballpoint into his pockets. The telephone rang and Caxton listened for a moment, said, "Twenty minutes. Right," then hung up.

Pickett said, "But you're not even involved anymore. It's Wilkie's problem now. Leave it that way."

"Yeah, well, that's what Betty says, too." There was no conviction in his voice. "Let me lock up now, Mel. Wilkie's coming and I have to get my boat and take them up to the cottages."

Feeling bundled out of the office, Pickett got into his car and pulled out of the driveway. In his rearview mirror, he watched Caxton come out of his house and look up and down the street, ignoring a greeting from Dr. Kuntz, standing in his drive two houses away. He had intended to ask Caxton if there was any way he could help—not with the investigation, of course, he wanted no part of that, but perhaps literally in the bakery. But Caxton clearly wanted no one around him. He was probably afraid that the killer would turn out to be someone he liked a lot more than he had liked Marlow.

Each of the cottages had its own dock, and the policemen tied up to each in succession as they searched their way along the shore. None of the cottages was locked, and a glance through each room was enough to tell whether it had been disturbed. While Wilkie checked the rooms, Copps and Caxton looked around outside.

"How big are the lots here?" Copps asked.

Caxton said, "They've got about a quarter of an acre each, but it's frontage that matters. A little piece of sand for young kids, an easy place to build a dock, that kind of thing."

"How far back do they go? The lots."

"You could probably still find the survey stake if you had all day. I don't know. See, nobody worries about a property line on the sides or the back, because it's useless land except for summer cottages. No one is about to build a fence. Let's see how far back we can get."

He led Copps straight back, away from the river, through dense scrub and then suddenly they were faced with a solid wall of rock about twenty feet high. Caxton turned and led them along the foot of the rock until it became lower and they could scramble onto the top. Above the wall they crossed a smooth curved expanse of rock to a huge split, a sharp-edged gap about ten feet across and at least fifteen feet deep. "See," Caxton said, as if he had been looking for just such a crack. "You fall down there, we wouldn't even hear you shout."

"Where's the trail from here?"

Caxton pointed farther back into the bush. "Over there. The land rises to meet the height we're standing on."

"Can we get to it?"

"Not from here. There's another big rock fault between us and the trail. The people don't bother. They come and go by boat. The trail is for hunters."

"So no one goes through the bush from the shore?"

"No. Oh, heck, you *can* get through just about anywhere, but you have to know to go a couple of hundred meters one way, and then jump up to the next level of rock and come back, really pick your way. It's just too much trouble."

Wilkie called out to them from the shore, and the three men moved to the next cottage. Each cottage had presented its own building problems. Some of the owners had had to build high above their neighbors in order to find a large, flat foundation. Others were set much farther back in the bush to get on land high enough to avoid flooding. "Even in daylight you have to know your way around," Caxton said, "if you don't want to break a leg."

Only two cottages showed any sign of being used. In all the others, the water lines had been drained, the propane disconnected, and the bedding put into storage.

"Who lives here?" Wilkie asked. He was standing in the doorway of a large cottage, part of an odd little row of buildings starting with a one-room shack near the shore, then behind it a larger cottage with a screen porch, and finally the big one, a three-bedroom cottage with an inside toilet.

"This is the Beavises' place. They started with that itty-bitty little shack and then kept building new ones behind as they got some money and the family got bigger."

"Look at this." Wilkie was standing in the door of the kitchen. The cupboards hung open and there was a mug and a half-full percolator on the counter. "I guess they haven't left for the season."

"I saw them driving home last weekend," Caxton

said. He tested the coffee grounds with his finger. "Still damp."

"After a week? See anything out of place?"

They searched all three cabins carefully. In the smallest one, used as a storeroom, they found a human nest—a sleeping bag, a cushion, an empty Coke bottle, and three cigarette butts.

"Kids," Caxton said, automatically.

"In one sleeping bag?" Copps picked up one of the cigarette butts. "Do kids round here roll their own?" He sniffed the end. "It isn't pot. Someone holed up here."

"Before or after?"

"I would think before. You wouldn't shoot someone, then look for a place to sleep nearby, would you? Or would you?" He took a plastic bag out of his pocket and emptied the tin lid with the cigarette butts into it.

"You got a map of the area, Lyman?"

"In the office."

"Let's finish up here and take a look at it."

Only one other cottage had not been closed, but it had been tidied and there was no sign that it had been used by an outsider.

"Who owns this?"

"Dakin," Caxton said. "The guy who wrote the play they're practicing. After he opened that bed-and-breakfast, he had to find somewhere quiet away from the phone. That's what I heard."

"Can you get from the cottages to this concession road?" Wilkie asked. The three men were in Caxton's office studying an aerial survey of the river shore.

"There's one place. There." Caxton put his finger on a spot behind one of the cottages. "See, you'd have to walk through the bush here to the trail, then go along the trail until you were behind the Cooks' place, there, and then go up to the road from there. But, see, there's the ravine behind the Cooks' place. You can't get up to the trail, let alone the road, not straight up."

"Might take some time to find the way if you didn't know it, but it could be done by someone who knew the area."

"Oh, sure. I could do it. So could Marlow."

Wilkie waited until he and Copps were alone in the car, ready to go home. "You see how this area works. For a stranger there's only one easy way in and out, along the trail. But if it *was* a stranger, he might not want to come running out of the bush after he shot Marlow. He might just find his way through to the Beavis cottage and stay the night. Wait until it's safe to come out."

"When would that be?"

"That would be hard for him to know, so he keeps his head down. Maybe by Sunday it looks safe, no search parties, nothing. Then two kids go for a walk and he has to go back into hiding."

Copps saw the point. "You think he's still around?"

"I don't know where he is; I don't know who he is. I don't know if he's a local or if he's a stranger. Marlow threw his weight around, I hear. Remember that town in the States where they shot the town bully in the cab of his pickup truck at high noon on market day, and they couldn't find any witnesses?"

"This is Ontario, boss, not the fucking Ozarks. Someone shot this guy because he was diddling his wife. Bet your life."

"Possibly. I don't want any surprises. We'll put a car down past the bridge, where we can watch the end of the trail. We'll put another one, a plain one, on that concession road."

On the way back to Sweetwater, Copps talked to Wilkie of another possibility. "Caxton was Betty Cullen's friend. Did you know that?"

"So I heard. Boyfriend, he told me."

"Kind of a dumb-looking peckerhead, but maybe we should check him out."

"How would we go about that?"

"How do you mean?"

"You say 'check him out.' What are you talking about? Find out who he is? I know who he is. Find out whether he had anything against Marlow? He hated the guy. So what's to check out? Fact is, 'check him out' doesn't mean fuck-all, it's bullshit from some TV show. When you get a real suggestion, let me know."

"Jesus, boss, I just mean the guy's a suspect."

"That, he is. So get him to show you around, get some idea of what makes him tick. I figure if you keep him with you, you can keep an eye on him. But go round on your own, too. Make up something that'll make the locals feel better. Tell the world you're looking for a drifter, someone who may have come to town any time recently but probably left on Friday night. Keep your ears open. Find out about Caxton's routine if he has one. I'll do the same, but see what people tell us about him. See if he's included in the people that the locals saw around on Friday. Find out what the locals think of him. Find out how big this rift was between him and Marlow."

"Big enough to put a body in?"

"That's more like it. And lighten up, for Christ's sake. He wasn't *your* brother."

"You really think Caxton might be involved?"

"The way Mel Pickett tells it, Caxton was surprised to find out whose body it was. As I said, *I* don't want any surprises."

CHAPTER 7

Pickett's last stop before supper was the Anglican Church hall, where Eliza was rehearsing her play.

When Pickett arrived at the rehearsal, only Eliza and Dennis Corning were still there, getting ready to leave. Eliza hurried forward as Pickett walked through the door. "We're just off," she said. "You go ahead, Dennis. I'll get Mel to drop me off. I have to talk to him about making a cupboard big enough to hide in."

Corning, looking as if this was news to him, shrugged, shook his head, shrugged again, then turned and left.

"Had a fight?" Pickett asked. "This morning upset you?"

"A bit. And we've had a bad afternoon. Did you know I'd given Dennis a little part? He's replacing the man who played one of the servants, who dropped out. This other man drives a truck for the highways department and he's been offered a lot of overtime on the weekends, so he won't be available. It's a tiny part but bloody Dennis is hopeless and we got into an argument about it."

"Never teach your wife to drive a car," Pickett said.

"What? Oh, I suppose so. That and some macho rubbish. And he disagrees with my direction. He's such an arrogant . . . All he has to do is stand there with his arms at his side and say things like, There's two men outside asking for you, and, Right you are, sir. But he keeps throwing himself about, acting. And he's put on this weird accent; he's not supposed to be English, the play takes place *here*; he's supposed to be a mill worker helping out for the night, but Dennis is talking like a Mississippi share-cropper with a speech impediment. A black one." Pleased with her wit, she smiled at herself, over the worst.

"It'll be all right on the night," Pickett said, the joke between them. He was not surprised. The morning had given Pickett some insight into Dennis Corning, and he suspected now that finding the body had been a defining moment in their relationship. He had read a story once in which the writer claimed that his hero, confronted with a sudden crucial test of courage, had passed the test and thereby instantly evolved from an unformed playboy into a man. He had admired the story when he read it, but it seemed simplistic to him now. What he had observed much more among adults he had come into contact with as a policeman was that in a crisis, a moment can occur in a relationship when one partner realizes the true nature of the other, his partner's essential strength or weakness, goodness or its opposite. The defining moment. The word Eliza was searching for was "prick."

"Not this year, it won't. And John, our playwright, broke down in tears halfway through his speech. Pat has left him."

"Pat Dakin? Gone?"

"Apparently. She says she can't stay in this place any

longer. She's been trying to write a novel, did you know? I think she's jealous of him, especially since she's found out *she* can't act, either. She's been writing at their cabin while he's been rehearsing and now she wants all her time to herself, so she's gone to Toronto to find a place of her own."

"She gone already?"

"Yesterday."

"What's the novel about?" Pickett asked. They were outside now, standing between their two vehicles.

"Oh, heaven knows. Herself, I would think. I don't know. Maybe the problem is menopause."

"It takes you in different ways," Pickett agreed, remembering his own wife. For a time she had lost interest in cooking and housekeeping, wanting no company and finding pleasure only in her garden, which she groomed fiercely for hours and which bloomed as she faded. She came through it eventually, but for a while the gap between them had frightened him badly.

"Maybe she's fallen for somebody else," he joked.

"At her age?"

"She still looks pretty nimble to me," Pickett said, irritated. "Anyway, what's it going to do to the play?"

"John Dakin wants to give it up. With her gone, he won't be able to keep the bed-and-breakfast place going. Too much of a strain, he says. And half of it belongs to her, and she wants her money back."

"This is all kind of quick, isn't it? I mean, did he unload this on all of you this afternoon? When did she announce that she was going?"

"He just told me. When he started crying, the rehearsal

broke up and I asked Dennis to get us some coffee, and Dakin let it all out. I hardly know the man but he went into this sort of wail as if we were old friends. It was so naked. I just sat and held his hand, saying 'there, there.' I think it's nice that men have learned to cry but I hope they hang on to a *bit* of the old restraint."

"It must have had a background, been building up for a while."

"Started when she left the play, probably. He even told me they don't sleep together. 'Cohabit,' he called it." She snorted.

"He told you?" Pickett was shocked.

"Yes, it reminded me of a time when my mother told me about the trouble she and Dad were having in bed. I remember thinking I was much too young to know things like that."

Pickett thought that every day with Eliza was a learning experience. "How will the others take it? Will they be disappointed after the work they've put in?"

"Oh, I'm not going to stop now. Dakin can't take his play, even if he goes back to Toronto. I won't let him. If necessary, *you'll* have to play the host."

Pickett laughed at the absurdity, then raised a question that had slightly puzzled him. "These people don't mind taking orders from you?" Eliza was twenty-five, pretty, with a very nice body, all of which might irritate the minister's wife, an Ottawa valley lady built like a fire hydrant.

"I haven't given any orders yet. At the moment I read out the stage directions and get them to face the front and speak up. That's enough for now. First, I have to find a new Tony Lumpkin. Any ideas?"

"Someone else quit?" So far, Pickett had acquired a very sketchy idea of what the play was about, and none at all of the characters.

"Sorry. That's what started the trouble today. Tony Lumpkin was played by the boys' high-school teacher from Sweetwater, but he's had to drop out because his wife objects to all the time he's away from home."

"She took a look at you, probably. Can you find anyone else?"

"I once thought of asking Timmy Marlow, believe it or not. He used to hang around, offering to help. You must have seen him occasionally, earlier in the summer. He watched us sort out some of the parts at the beginning. We never had a Lumpkin for a long time; Dakin used to read the part because he's not on stage much with him, at first, but then it got awkward, and I thought of asking Marlow, and then this schoolteacher appeared, and he was good at the part and helpful to me. Now I'm stuck again. By the way, we don't have to stop everything out of some kind of respect, do we?"

"I'd say the show must go on. Why was Marlow hanging around in the first place?"

"I don't know. Curiosity, maybe." Her manner indicated that she knew very well.

"You?"

"Me?"

"I hear he was always on the prowl."

"Oh, Mel." She laughed. "That's another play, called *Lock Up Your Daughters*. He wasn't after me, not that I could tell. No more me than anyone else. He tried, like he did with everybody, but I saw him coming. His technique was a bit off-putting. It consisted of talking dirty and closing up on you from behind. I knew a boy like that when I was fifteen. He was a creep."

Pickett could not stop himself. "What do you mean, talking dirty?"

"You know perfectly well. The kind of thing you usually get in a work situation with five or six men and one woman. He did it all by himself. Dirty compliments mostly. Lots of puns. He probably thinks that's what they mean by oral sex."

Pickett let it go. "What are you going to do? Any ideas?"

"Do you know someone called Craig Thompson? Works in the hardware store?"

"I've seen him. The son."

"He does Benny Hill impersonations, apparently. He's my only hope." She leaned her back against the car door. "You think I should call it off, Mel?"

"You'll have to ask yourself that one. Let's get you home now."

"I'll give it a last try. You know, little bits of it sound quite real." She opened the door of his car. "Are you okay for supper? You could eat with us, if you like."

"No, thanks. I've been invited out. Ask me again, though. I'm going to stay up for the week. The weather's promised to be good enough for me to finish the deck." He climbed into the driver's seat.

When they reached her door, she said, "I'll come and look for you during the week."

"You'll probably find me in my cabin, writing a novel, like everyone else around here."

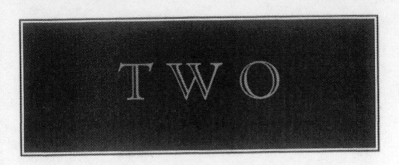

CHAPTER 8

"There's been a lot of guessing," Charlotte Mercer said, just before supper on the same day. "People are falling over themselves trying to figure which husband might have done it. They reckon Marlow could've run foul of any of half a dozen of them, and a few other people besides. People have been asking me if I know anything."

"Why you?"

"Don't play dumb."

"They should ask the OPP." He knew what she meant, of course. Pickett's background was common knowledge, and the town had watched him all day, close to the investigation. And Pickett's admiration for Charlotte was common knowledge.

"Have a little rest now," Charlotte said. "I have to make gravy. I'll call you when dinner's ready. Turn round." She pushed his shoulder to make him turn over. "God, you're a big bugger," she said. She ran her hand over his head to make the remark friendly, giving the thick white bristles a tug.

"You had to be when I joined. They changed that, though, so as not to discriminate." Pickett closed his eyes as she slid out of bed. She did not like to be looked at after they had made love, though she didn't mind before, probably because she felt he would be less critical then. Pickett liked what he saw at any time, but he honored her diffidence.

It had been clear to him after the tenth or eleventh visit to the coffee shop that he had something going with Charlotte, or might have, or could have. In fact, even with every scrap of circumspection he could bring to bear, a prudence compounded of abstinence, a desire to avoid late-middle-age foolishness, and a distrust of what, after all, might be no more than a firefly glow at twilight, he found himself courting her.

It began with a shared cup of coffee whenever he came into the restaurant; this turned into a daily visit and then her offer to cook his Sunday supper the weekend she knew he was working hard to try to get the windows installed. It might have taken them a year to get to the next square, but then Pickett, by way of apology for his appearance at Sunday supper, mentioned the inadequacy of the washing facilities in his trailer—a pan of warm water was all he could manage then—so that he couldn't clean up properly before supper with her and stayed gritty for the long drive back to Toronto afterward. She pointed out that she had a perfectly good bathroom and could probably lend him a towel if she was pushed. Still Pickett hung back, not sure of country ways and not wanting to upset the good thing he already had going, until the third or fourth weekend he came out of the bathroom and found her sitting on the edge of the bed in the room where he changed, looking nervous. Later on she said she had tried everything else and if that didn't lead to anything, she was going to tell him to eat somewhere else.

That first time was alarming, and brief, but it was also terrific because she said she didn't care, just having someone close to her again was enough, and as for him, just holding a woman he liked and being held in return was a pleasure he had nearly forgotten. Thereafter, even after his cabin was finished and his own washing arrangements had improved, though not to the point of a shower, he still arrived dirty on Sunday evening. Otherwise they would have had to invent a whole new dance to get into bed, and he liked coming out of the shower and finding her in bed, waiting to spend their half hour under the duvet before dinner, learning how much autumn still had left for them.

As far as they knew it was a secret. The town knew only that they were friends. Charlotte was fiercely concerned to keep it so, not so much because of her good name but because she disliked anyone knowing anything about her private life. Pickett simply held his breath, struck with his good fortune and alive to every signal from Charlotte about the right decorum to use to protect their passion. He understood that no one these days, even in Larch River, was really interested anymore in lovemaking between unencumbered adults, even elderly ones, but if secrecy was what Charlotte wanted, he was certainly happy to play along, and he never suggested staying the night.

He scratched his belly and stretched out luxuriously under the duvet. He wondered how they would go on from here. Pickett had lived for long enough on his own that he had formed the habit of reflection, and one of the things he reflected about now was that it might not get any better than this. Sometimes it seemed like a powerful pessimistic streak, the conviction that there was nothing better to look forward to, but Pickett saw it as simply not postponing the present for the sake of the future, seizing the day, as it were. He had spent long enough when things were not as good as this, thinking that was normal and the way it was always going to be, not to know when things were good.

Age gave you self-consciousness; you never quite lost yourself even during the best of times, and while this meant that you could never feel immortal again, that time itself never stopped or even slowed down, it also meant that nothing good slipped by, or was taken for granted. Here now, he had just made love and been made love to by a lady who made him feel better—more at home, was how he put it to himself—than he thought anyone ever would again. He thought about her when he was working on the cabin, and he knew by the things she said when he walked into the café that she did the same. And pretty soon he would go downstairs and eat roast chicken, potatoes, carrots, and broccoli. (He hated broccoli, but Charlotte insisted that there had to be a green vegetable, and not peas every time. Everything else would be as good as roast chicken dinners got.)

The thing was, it was a regular date now. Every Sunday, sex—no, he was beginning to dislike that word, the all-licensed term with its connotations of bodily parts and mechanical aids (the word even sounded like a lubricant) and all the sleaze of rows of *XXXX*'s, and a woman on television teaching techniques ("do not try to get the whole membair in ze mouth all at once")— no, every Sunday, a nice bonk, and then a roast dinner. And during the week, a half hour a day in the coffee shop, touching base (touching hands), trying not to act like a kid. But he knew it couldn't last, because nothing never changed, so along with telling yourself that this, now, was as good as it would get, you had to be aware of the fact that it would end. Although Charlotte had so far given no sign that she saw their arrangement as temporary, or needing to progress, time would bring change. The thing was to try to control the change so as to have the best that the future could offer. The thing was to try to analyze the present to discover how much the contentment he was feeling now, under this duvet, depended on the particular arrangement they had; whether the half hour a day and the Sunday get-together did not constitute a very finely balanced relationship that allowed them the best of each other; or whether they should get married.

They hadn't talked about it. Would she understand if he tried to set up a conversation about it? Would he be able to find the language to point out the risks they might be taking, that more of each other's company might mean less, though he didn't know that? That was what they needed to find out. There was a lot to think through.

Charlotte called from downstairs, rousing him. "You've got time for a beer," she called. "But only just."

He dressed and went downstairs to the beer she had

already opened. She continued to bustle for a few minutes, then joined him with an empty glass, holding it out for some of his beer. "Just a little," she said. "There."

"Why don't you get one of your own?"

"I only want a little."

Pickett looked at his half-empty bottle, repressing the desire to say that he had looked forward to a whole bottle. If he was going to live with her they would have to get this straight.

She said, "I bought a bottle of wine. Shall we have some?"

"Not for me. You go ahead. I like it on its own, but not with food. I'll have another beer, though."

"You'll get fat."

Love chat. Slightly proprietary, too. A little of it was all right, Pickett thought, but in fairness they ought to talk soon, about what it meant.

She put the beer down in front of him. "How'd your friend Eliza make out after? Did you go down to the play practice?"

"She had a bad afternoon. Her rehearsals went wrong. One of the actors quit."

"Did they know about Timmy Marlow?"

"Sure, but I don't think he was connected to any of them. He used to hang around sometimes."

"Checking out Eliza. Was he coming on to her?"

"She says not."

"Who else would he be interested in?"

"There's just Donna McMurtry, the minister's wife."

Charlotte laughed. "That I'd like to see. Who can Eliza get for the one who's quit?"

"Someone suggested Craig Thompson over at the hardware store. You know him?"

"He'd be good. He's always joking around, imitating things on television."

Pickett said, "When did Marlow come here? You told me once."

"Betty and Sam opened the bakery about fifteen years ago; then maybe five years later, Sam died. She ran it by herself, and Lyman Caxton helped when they started to get together. Up until then she'd been kind of an outsider, but people wanted to help out when Sam went."

"Where did they come from? Why did they choose this place?"

"Betty told me Sam used to run a little radio station out in Manitoba somewhere, but it got bought up by a big chain and Sam was out of a job. She said he was tired of it anyway, and he wanted to do something different, so they took a little trip up through here and saw the bakery advertised for sale in the Lindsay paper . . . These damn corkscrews are no good. Look at that; it's good wine, too. Imported." She surveyed the mess of broken cork still jammed in the neck of the bottle.

"Here." Slowly, carefully he slid the cork out.

"How'd you do that?"

"You have to press it tight to the side of the bottle. Waiter showed me once."

"Great. Usually I get the sharpening iron and push it all the way in."

"Then it shoots up your arm and you have to pour it through a Kleenex to filter out the bits of cork. And you have to drink it all."

"No, you don't. I have a rubber gizmo you can use as a plug. You can use it in beer bottles, too. Drink half a bottle now and save a half until tomorrow."

"I'll remember if I ever want six ounces of beer all at one go. So tell me more."

She put the wine bottle down and dabbed at a pool of spilled wine on the counter. "Where was I? Yeah. We'd been without a baker for a couple of months after Phyllis had to give it up, but there was always a good living there, especially in the summer, of course." She laughed. "You can sell anything to Toronto people if it's homemade. Old Mrs. Grosskurth makes the worst apple and blueberry pies you've ever tasted, but she sells hundreds off a table outside her house. Where was I? Yes. Let's see, Timmy wasn't around when I started the coffee shop. Did you know that was my idea? Percy Harlan wanted me to pump gas on the weekend, after my husband died, but I persuaded him to build the coffee shop instead. Makes more money than the gas pumps now. What was I saying? The coffee shop was built eight years ago, and Timmy appeared shortly after."

"From where?"

"Somewhere out west. The whole family's from Manitoba. There's peach pie for dessert. Fresh peaches. Want some ice cream? You probably shouldn't."

Once again Pickett felt that the line between concern for him and taking him over was being eroded. Was she just a little bit bossy? If he agreed with her, would she move on to something else she thought would be good for him? "I'll have some ice cream," he said.

She didn't react at all. It was just a remark. They

were both set in their ways. There wasn't a lot of room for change. So what would he lose if he moved in here? He knew what he would gain. He had just enjoyed it. So go ahead, or back up? Wait and see. He was pretty sure, though, that Charlotte would not remain his Sunday afternoon girlfriend indefinitely. There was simply no other word for it; they were courting. What they were doing on Sunday afternoons used to be called bundling, if you kept your clothes on. It was a very nice thing to have happen to him so late in life.

While she was bringing him his pie, he thought about Timmy Marlow hanging around the rehearsals, and now Charlotte's comment seemed apt. It wasn't the theater that interested Marlow, and since Eliza had not mentioned any other woman except Donna McMurtry he *must* have been after Eliza. It seemed unlikely that she would not have been aware of it, but as she told it, his pass at her was purely routine. He must remember to ask her again.

CHAPTER 9

On his way home, he saw the light on in Caxton's office and tried not to notice, but Caxton was sitting at his desk, looking out the window. Pickett waved, and Caxton stood to wave back, so Pickett was more or less obliged to stop. Caxton met him at the door. "Come in for a nightcap, Mel? I could use the company."

Pickett walked through into the living room and sat down, wondering what he had let himself in for. He did not think of Caxton as a serious drinker, but the half-full bottle of rye was open on the coffee table, and Caxton's glass was in his hand. Caxton poured Pickett a giant drink and added ginger ale, all without asking, then handed him the glass. Pickett, who hated rye and ginger ale, wet his lips and sat back.

"He's done it to me, Mel, like I told you. He had to get killed to do it, but he's done it. She's leaving."

"Betty? When?"

"Soon as she can sell the bakery. Maybe before. She's closing the shop and going."

"This is just day one. She'll feel different in the morning."

"I doubt it. But even if she does, I think he's screwed

us up." He dropped his head, then slowly raised it until he was looking closely at Pickett's face. Pickett wondered how drunk he was, and what kind of a drunk he would turn out to be. "What happened?" he asked, to have something to say.

Caxton focused on him, his eyes blinking as if against a strong light. "She doesn't want me to come around anymore."

"But . . ."

"*But, but*, no fucking *but*s, she just told me to get lost."

"In those words?"

"Yes. No. What's the difference?"

Pickett started to speak, but Caxton waved him silent. This was a monologue. "You know, finally I thought things were going good. I was married once, until one of the guys told me she was fucking everybody in the district. After that I could never find a steady, you know what I mean?" He waited until Pickett nodded. He knew what Caxton meant. "Mostly, you know, hookers, and then nothing. Then I met Betty again when I came here. Took a long time for us to get together, but it was worth it. She wouldn't move in with me but she came over here, know what I mean?" Pickett nodded again. "We were going to get married soon. Just about to announce it, we were. You were on the list to come to the wedding. Not now. Not now. She says when they find out who did it, everyone will blame Timmy as much as the guy who killed him. So she's leaving."

"It doesn't make much sense. But go with her. Start up again."

"Don't you think I offered?" Caxton's face came closer.

Easy now, Pickett thought. This guy wants to hit someone. But Caxton quieted down with his next words.

"She won't have me. Says we'd better break it up now. She says she won't be responsible for me giving up everything that I've got here. But what have I got if she goes?" Caxton pulled out a desk drawer and emptied it on the floor. "Garbage is what I've got. Pile of garbage."

"Why don't I make some coffee, Lyman?"

Caxton seemed not to hear. "You know, when I left Lands and Forests everything turned to rat shit, until I came here. Then gradually it started to go right. When they made me chief, I was as happy as I've ever been. Betty was the clincher. Now she's going. If that son of a bitch wasn't already dead, I'd kill him myself."

"Easy." Pickett racked his brains in an effort to turn Caxton onto a narrative path, away from his misery. "You said you met Betty again. Did you know her before somewhere?"

Caxton looked at Pickett from a long way away, trying to get the focus right. "Didn't I tell you? We met at a dance in Kenora years ago when I was working in the Keewatin district. She was on holiday there. But she already had a boyfriend in Winnipeg, so I never saw her again. I didn't forget, though, nor did she." He paused to keep his narrative straight. "Jesus, it was all going so well, you know? She'd just told Timmy he had to move out of the house, and if he would move away, even to Sweetwater, so as not to be a problem for me, she would have helped him out until he found a job. With him out of the way, we could get married. Now he's dead, and she keeps saying she's afraid of what might come out."

"Does she think he was involved in something crooked around here?"

"She's just afraid."

"Did she know where he was this weekend? Did she know he was missing?"

"He told her he was going to Toronto. Says he acted like he was going to some woman. Maybe he was. But he didn't get there. Maybe he met someone's husband along the way."

"She must have been shocked."

"Not at first." Caxton adopted a wry expression much magnified by his drunkenness. "I tried to break it to her gently. I told her they'd found a guy dead on the trail. You know what she said? 'Timmy didn't do it.' When I told her it was Timmy who was dead, she didn't react at all. Not at first. Later on she started to cry about her poor Timmy, but not right away. Then when I went back there tonight, she'd already made up her mind. She said she'd had time to think it over and if Timmy was killed up on that trail, then it was a local, and probably something to do with a woman, and when it all came out she wouldn't want to live here anymore. So she's going now. When I tried to tell her what a good-for-nothing, sponging bastard he was, always in rut, she started in on me. 'He was my brother and he was all I had,' she said, kind of shouting, 'You've never liked him, and you're glad he's dead. So go.' I never heard her shout before. What'll I do, Mel? This is my whole life, right here."

"Stay, then."

"With her gone?" Caxton's face twisted in misery.

And then, for all his sympathy, Pickett felt bored and tired. And embarrassed. He was not Caxton's friend, and yet here he was being thrust into the role, because there was no one else. Pickett thought of himself as a loner; before Charlotte he often thought he knew about loneliness. But he could think of at least three people apart from Charlotte who cared what happened to him, and then, in his new contentment, he was flooded with pity for Caxton, who thought he had found someone like that, only to have her evaporate. "Don't sit here drinking, Lyman," he said. "I have to get home and let the dog out. Come home with me. Have some coffee. Stay at my place if you like."

"She means it, I'm telling you."

"Wait and see."

It wasn't going to be easy to get away. Pickett resigned himself to sit it out, and tasted his drink again. Then he said, "I forgot. I'm allergic to this stuff. You got any scotch?"

Caxton shook his head. "Got some cognac. Betty liked cognac."

"Where is it? I'll get it."

Back in his chair with something drinkable, Pickett said, "Where did Betty come from? Before she moved here."

Caxton squinted at him. "Barrie. Yeah, Barrie. That's where she got married. Then her husband wanted to open his own business and they heard of the bakery up here."

"When was this?"

"Fifteen years ago?"

"She was from Manitoba originally, right? Where-abouts?"

"She was born in Dauphin. She left home early, when she was about seventeen. Because of her old man."

Pickett braced himself for yet another story of incest. But it was a more conventional brutality that Caxton was referring to.

"He was a drunk. Beat her up sometimes. Kept taking her money. So she went off to Winnipeg, on her own."

"And Timmy?"

"He stayed home. He was just a kid. Then her mother died and Betty went back to look after her brother. When he was old enough, he took off on his own and she went back to Winnipeg, but then she came east to get away from the old man. He had a bad habit of turning up on her doorstep in Winnipeg, drunk. He froze to death in the end. Drove his pickup into a ditch in the middle of winter."

All this was helping. Talking seemed to calm Caxton down. Pickett tried again. "Where will she go now?"

"She won't say. She won't tell me."

"So go to bed and think about it tomorrow."

"She means it, Mel."

For Christ's sake. "So believe her. She's gone. You have to start again. But not tonight. Tonight you have to go to bed. And I have to get back to let the dog out. I've been away too long as it is."

But it took another hour. By that time Caxton had

drunk the last third of the bottle of rye, and Pickett persuaded him to lie down on the couch and take his shoes off. When he passed out, Pickett turned off the lights and drove home to Willis.

Caxton called him the next morning as he was finishing his breakfast. "Was I being an asshole last night?" he wanted to know.

"No more than usual."

"I told you about Betty, eh?"

"Yes, you did."

"I just wrote her a letter. Told her how much I've appreciated her over the last few years."

Jesus.

"That sounds good," Pickett said. "But don't send it off right away. Let it cook for a day or so."

"Why?"

"Just to be sure it's what you want to do. Last night you were . . . smashed. This morning you're suffering. Wait until you feel normal."

"That sounds like good advice. You've got a real head on you, Mel. That wasn't what I called you for, though. See, Wilkie wanted me to drive Betty in to do the ID. I don't want to do that now. Would you mind?"

"Tell Wilkie to send a car."

"She asked me if I would ask you to take her in."

"Why? I don't even know her except to see."

"I've told her about you and that cabin you're building. She asked me."

"Okay. What time?"

"Now."

"All right. I'll have to wash. I'll be there in half an hour."

Pickett thought, When they ask you, you have to go, especially if they have no one else to ask.

The sign on the door of the bakery was turned to CLOSED. Betty Cullen came out as he pulled up in front of the store and stepped immediately into the car. Pickett turned onto the highway to Sweetwater. He waited for some indication from her that she wanted to talk, but they drove in silence until they reached the edge of Sweetwater. Then she said, "I guess you think I'm being hard on Lyman."

So that was why he was driving her. She wanted to get a message to him, and probably through him to Caxton. He said, "You're having a rough time. I don't have any opinions on how you should be. You have to do what you feel like."

"I won't be able to stay here after they find out who killed Timmy."

"Why don't you wait and see? Could have been a stranger. Anyway, people won't blame you."

"They'll point me out to each other."

"For a few . . ."

"Look," she interrupted him fiercely, "I know what I'm going to do. I'm going to get rid of the bakery and go somewhere else. I've thought about it enough. But Lyman hasn't done anything. He's got a good life here, and it's not fair that he should have to give it up."

"Maybe he would want to."

"I'm not letting him. Best for him that we finish now.

But I didn't ask you to drive me in for that. I just wanted to ask you to be a pal to him. Would you? He thinks a lot of you, and he doesn't have any buddies. That's partly his job, I suppose, but he's always been more or less on his own. He needs someone to talk to, I know that. So I thought I'd tell you how much he admires you and maybe you could spend a little time with him. For a while."

It was naked, embarrassing, and naive in its assumptions about relationships. How could he explain to her that he and Caxton had no history on which to base a friendship, that it wasn't something you could just initiate if it hadn't happened in the past three years? And then he thought that she wasn't asking him to be bosom pals with Caxton. Just to keep an eye on him and listen to him occasionally. In other words, be a neighbor. He could do that.

"I'll look him up," he said. He added, "If he stays around."

"Tell him to," she said again, with a fierceness that surprised him. "Talk him out of leaving. Where would he go?"

Pickett pulled into the parking lot of the OPP detachment in Sweetwater and offered a thought. "You're leaving because of the shame of it all, or some such, aren't you? Don't you think he might have trouble with that, too? He might not want to carry on being chief, might think that he's tainted. He could well want to make a clean break."

"Tell him not to," she said. "Tell him to forget about me."

★　　　　★　　　　★

They met Wilkie in his office, and he drove ahead of them to the little hospital where Marlow's body was being kept in cold storage.

"Let me go first," Wilkie said. "I'll put the light on and you can go in when I come out. It's pretty bad, you know that."

She stood close to the door, waiting for the moment to go in. "I don't want anyone watching me," she said.

She came out almost immediately, nodded, and turned away, trembling slightly.

Pickett took her arm and led her back to the car. When he had helped her inside, he came back to Wilkie, who was standing by his own car. "She'll want to know the schedule," he said. "When can she think of a funeral?"

"There's an autopsy, an inquest—I don't know. Not until we're sure what happened. Why are you driving her around?"

Pickett explained briefly her desire to keep Caxton out of any unpleasantness.

"Bit excessive, isn't it?"

"Maybe not for her. I'll do what I can."

"Who shot him, Mel?"

"Everyone in Larch River is hoping it was a stranger."

"You have to, don't you?"

By the time Pickett had returned to the car she was composed enough to ask him to stop at a grocery store on the main street of Sweetwater. "I don't want to be stared at, shopping in Larch River," she reminded him. She seemed to be surviving her ordeal well enough now.

He waited at the door of the store to help carry her grocery bags to the car. They said nothing on the ride back. Pickett was feeling himself being sucked into Caxton's world by the sheer pull of the man's need of him, and he wanted to preserve some distance. He felt uneasy. There was no way of knowing where the investigation might lead, and while the idea of Lyman Caxton as a killer was absurd, his training told him that Wilkie couldn't think that way. He did not want to be privy to any of Caxton's secrets that Wilkie ought to know.

Betty unlocked the door of the bakery and stepped in, turning in the doorway to take the groceries from him. He was very conscious of Lyman Caxton sitting in his car, watching the house from a block away. In spite of wanting to stay clear, he would have to find an excuse to drop by; Caxton, it seemed to him, was capable of getting emotional enough to do something silly, like trying to hunt down the killer all by himself.

CHAPTER 10

On Tuesday, the Larch River *Gazette* carried an account of the incident, together with a picture of Marlow. The *Gazette* was not much more than an advertising flyer, but it was widely distributed in the area, and a man in Jacob's Creek, a hamlet eight miles from Larch River, recognized Marlow's picture and called in to the OPP in Sweetwater.

The duty constable led him through to Wilkie's office.

"I saw your guy," the man said. "The dead guy. He was in one of those cottages up past the landing."

"When?"

"Three weeks ago? Hold on." The man, Jerry Laker, a salesman of camping supplies and sporting goods, thumbed through a small diary. "The hardware store in Larch River carries our stuff and I did an order there in the morning and then took a few hours off to go fishing. I do that a lot if I've met my quota. Here it is, Wednesday the eleventh. I rented a boat at the marina and went up to the fishing camp. I know the good spots along there and I was planning to fish my way back.

"So I'm most of the way home, trolling the shoreline,

and I ran out of gas. Son of a bitch at the marina hadn't filled up the tank—there's no way I could've used five gallons. We had a little argument about it when I got in." He grinned. "It's nice to tell an asshole what he is, after you've spent a week being polite, kissing butts to get an order. Anyway, there I was, up shit creek. I did have a paddle but it's slow going, paddling a sixteen-foot aluminum boat, so I was hoping someone would come by and give me a tow. Then I saw smoke coming from the chimney of one of the cottages, and I thought I would see if I could borrow a gallon of gas. I tied up at the dock and unhooked my gas tank, but just as I was getting out of the boat, this guy came out of the cabin. He couldn't see me, so I stayed where I was until he was back inside the cabin."

"What was he doing?"

"He was taking a leak in the bushes around the side of the cabin. He'd come out to use the outhouse, I guess, but he couldn't be bothered to walk that far. He was nearly naked, just had his shorts on, so it was a bit awkward for me. Once he was back inside, I stepped out onto the dock and hollered, real loud, Anybody home? Then I walked, real slow, up to the cottage, hollering every few steps. Your guy opened the door as I got to the porch. He was more or less dressed now. I'm sure it was him because of his stupid little beard. Behind him, in the living room, I could see a young girl, maybe sixteen or seventeen, watching me, pretending to read a maga-zine. She made a hell of an impression on me, too, because although I couldn't see her face because of the magazine, I could sure see the rest of her. She was wearing some kind of bathrobe that was mostly open and she had her feet up on the little table in front of her, posing like a picture in a skin magazine. Apart from that, all I could see of her was her long yellow hair."

All this, Wilkie, as good as his word, reported to Pickett on his way through Larch River that afternoon. He continued, "Caxton identified her right away. Linda McCourt. She works behind the desk of that gas station up at the junction, the big new one. Her old man owns it. So I went up to see her.

"She was scared of her old man finding out at first, so I had to explain that I didn't have any interest in her sex life, though between ourselves it could have been interesting. She's a feisty little babe—I had the feeling she was measuring me while we were talking. Anyway, I told her that officially, in case her old man wondered, I was inquiring if she had seen any suspicious characters on foot near the gas station, or walking the highway to and from Larch River, and then she agreed that she and Marlow had spent the occasional afternoon at the Dakin cottage, just a couple of times, but apart from the man who came looking for gas, whom she remembered, no one had seen them, she was sure. Marlow used to pick her up at a government dock around the point, the place canoeists use as a starting point for their trips. They got to the cottage by boat, and afterward he took her back to the government dock, where she had left her car. Not on weekends, no. On her afternoon off. The last time they'd spoken to each other was in early August, she said, when they had a fight.

"I asked her what the fight was about, and she said

they had an arrangement to spend a couple of days in Toronto together. They were going to drive in separately and meet at a hotel in Toronto. He never turned up, never called, nothing. When she came back, she went over to the bakery to find him, and he told her he'd left a message at the hotel to say he couldn't make it. Anyway, he said it wasn't his problem. She should have been more careful."

"About what?"

"She went in to have an abortion, which she had, without anyone around to hold her hand. If her father had found out, he'd have wanted to kill someone—her or Marlow. So that was their last date. She said when she heard he'd been shot she assumed it was because he had been caught screwing around with someone else. Anyway, she was glad. She said it wasn't her problem. He should have been more careful."

"Does her father own a handgun?" Pickett joked.

"Does Linda McCourt have a jealous boyfriend her own age?" Wilkie pondered in return.

"I'd say not. If she was screwing a character like Marlow—how old was he, thirty?—then that's where she got her kicks. She'd regard boys her own age as kids."

"That's what I figured. She's frightened of her old man, of course, but she couldn't help bragging a little that she was Marlow's mistress, even though he'd dumped her like that."

"Does she think she was the only one?"

"Wasn't she?" Wilkie asked.

"From what Lyman Caxton tells me, Marlow spread himself around. The history includes two others around here that Caxton knows about. He covered a lot of territory delivering bread, until his sister took some of the flak and put a stop to it. He got caught by the guy who runs the campers' supply store at the junction just outside of town. This guy had gone to Toronto for a fresh supply of that junk he sells, the moccasins made in Taiwan, and decided for a change not to stay over as he usually did. He came home and found his missus in bed with Marlow. He phoned Betty Marlow and told her to take him off the bread route. Told her why."

"So far, then, it could have been a drinking pal, a husband, or maybe a jilted lady."

"The most likely is someone with a grudge who'd lost a fight with Marlow. Marlow liked to fight, too."

Wilkie held out his mug for more coffee. "Can I leave out *anybody* around here?"

"Me. I never spoke to the guy. You say he and this kid used the Dakin cottage? You talked to Dakin yet? He and his wife run the bed-and-breakfast place on Main Street. He wrote a play they're putting on here. By the way, do many of the folks here have cottages as well as houses?"

"A few. The cottage is a place to take the kids on the holidays, I guess. And they rent them out. But, sure, I talked to Dakin. He hasn't used his cottage for a month. Apparently he let his wife use it so that she could be alone on the weekends. She was writing a book, he says."

"Where was Mrs. Dakin on Friday? If she was at the cottage she might have heard something." Pickett told Wilkie about the marriage breakup.

"Dakin never said anything about that. Where will I find her, do you know?"

"According to young Eliza, the girl who found the body, she left town on Saturday. What have you found out about Marlow? When was he last seen?"

"He left town on Friday afternoon. We'll know where he went when we find his car. It shouldn't be hard to spot. Rusted-out light blue Chevy. I've got the boys looking for it." Wilkie sat back. "So you know this Eliza? How?"

Pickett told him how.

"And this Dakin wrote the play you're all acting in?"

"I'm building the scenery. Dakin wrote the play, yeah."

"And Mrs. Dakin? She the one who serves frozen croissants?"

"That's the one."

"You're really in touch, aren't you? Stay close, all right?"

The car turned up the next day, tucked away on a quiet back street of Dumpy Lake, a resort village about fifteen miles away. Neither Betty nor Caxton had any idea what Marlow might have been doing in Dumpy Lake. Just as interesting was how he got back to Larch River. Wilkie had the car towed back to Sweetwater until he could make sense of it.

Caxton said, "I've been thinking, Mel."

Pickett felt a heavy depression in his chest. He had been putting in a shelf above the stove, a nice morning's work, when Caxton appeared. It looked as though he could expect a daily visit from Caxton while he worked out his misery. He could guess how it would go: every day Caxton would come to a conclusion about his relationship with Betty, a conclusion that Pickett would agree with, until the next day, when Caxton would see it all differently. This was more neighborliness than Pickett thought he might be able to cope with. "What about?" he asked.

"Did you ever see Marlow to remember?"

This sounded better. "Sure. I don't think I ever spoke to the guy, but I saw him around, and in the bakery, of course."

Caxton took a copy of the *Gazette* out of his jacket. "That what he looked like?"

"Yeah. That's him. Says so right there."

"Look at it hard, Mel. That the way you remember him?"

Pickett took the newspaper over to the light from the window. "Yes," he said. "He had that little beard. That's him."

"That's how the guy identified him, too, Wilkie told me, the guy who saw him in the cottage. 'Stupid little beard,' he said."

"So what's the point?"

"You couldn't really tell much from the look I took, but he didn't have a beard when we found him on the trail."

"Tell me what you're saying."

"Why would he shave off his beard?"

"He was bored with it. Wanted a change." Pickett abandoned the shelf for the day and turned on the stove ring to make coffee.

"Could be. Strange, though, don't you think? And Wilkie's not stupid. At some point he's going to wonder where the beard is. And if that fella who first saw him in the gully sees the picture in the paper, he might wonder, too."

"So what's on your mind, Lyman?"

"All right, I'll tell you, and you see if you can think of anything you haven't told me that either fits or don't fit. I think Timmy went up into the bush to meet someone. I mean, what if he went up there to have it out with someone?"

"Who?"

"I don't know. But it's strange, isn't it?"

"He had a shave, is all," Pickett said. "The rest you made up."

"Could be. I hated that goddamn beard. It was like the kind Abraham Lincoln had, you know? He was always stroking it, curling it up. I saw a woman in a beer parlor stroking it once with her finger; you could tell he was having her, just the way she did it."

"He's dead now, Lyman."

"Yeah, and he's screwed me up totally." He paused and looked out at Pickett's yard. "I think I'll find out about that beard, though."

He came back in triumph, early in the afternoon. "Don't tell me there's nothing strange going on," he began, excited, full of news. "You know what I found out? He shaved that beard off before he went up the trail on Friday."

"Who saw him?"

"No one *saw* him. I just . . . established it."

Pickett waited patiently for Caxton to shape the story for its full effect. He would get nothing done this afternoon.

"I drove over to Dumpy Lake after I left you," Caxton began. "You know why?"

"That's where they found Marlow's car."

"Right. There's three motels in Dumpy Lake. Marlow stayed in one of them, I found out."

"What for?"

"I reckon he went somewhere to get a shave."

Before Pickett could laugh, Caxton continued. "I was right. He took a room in the second one I checked. They recognized his picture. And I didn't even have to ask. They said he checked in early in the afternoon and left before supper, while it was still light. They figured he must have wanted someplace to take a woman, yet when they cleaned the room the next morning—he had to pay for the whole night, of course—the bed hadn't been used. But the thing they did notice was that the washbasin was full of hair. He'd shaved his beard off. What do you make of that?"

"I told you. He was bored with it."

"I've got a better idea. They didn't actually see any woman with Marlow. They just assumed that's what he was doing. I don't think there was one. I think he went to Dumpy Lake to shave off his beard and come back here without it."

"Why, for Christ's sake?"

"To change his appearance. Because he didn't want to be recognized by anyone as he came through town. He came back here and waited up on the trail. But the other guy was too smart for him. What do you think?"

"I don't know what to say. It's ingenious, I'll agree with that. You going to tell Wilkie?"

"No."

"Maybe you should."

"And maybe I shouldn't. Mr. OPP Wilkie has as good as told me to keep out of it. He lets me watch, is all, just in case I see something he might miss."

Pickett knew why. Wilkie wanted Caxton where he could see him, but not part of the investigation. "What about the car?" he asked. "They found Marlow's car at Dumpy Lake. So how did he get back here?"

"I haven't worked that out yet."

"Most of what you've told me is just speculating. But if you come across anything concrete, you have to let Wilkie know."

A car turned into the yard, Eliza's Volkswagen. Caxton stood up with the slightly inflated air of a man who would divulge what he knew in his own sweet time.

Pickett said, "You don't have to go, Lyman. You know Eliza. I'll make some coffee."

"Something I want to look at," Caxton said. He made a hat-touching gesture at Eliza and climbed into his car. "I'll see you later."

"Did I interrupt?" Eliza asked, watching Caxton's car disappear through the gate.

"We weren't doing anything. Want some coffee?"

"Did I hear you say *beer?*"

Now *she* wants to talk to someone, Pickett thought. There goes the day. But he was retired and he couldn't think of anyone he would rather waste his time with.

He brought out two bottles of beer, leading the way to the picnic table.

"What's up?" he asked, to get her going. He was actually pleased and flattered that she had chosen him for whatever problem she wanted help with. She wouldn't drop by just to chat. Something had to be wrong. Dennis, of course.

She came to the point with her usual directness. "Let's see. First of all, I just told Dennis he can't write. Not films, anyway. That turned into an argument about my competence to say that, and my general competence to do my own job. Then we learned that I had a deep-rooted jealousy of creativity. You can tell by my editorial comments. Then we realized that my jealousy is what lies behind my need to cut his balls off, and that our lovemaking has deteriorated because he anticipates a criticism of his performance in that area, too, which naturally becomes a self-fulfilling prophecy. We had a fight, you might say."

"All because . . . ?"

"All because I told him his script was a pile of crap. Which it is." Her eyes were damp, but she was smiling, almost laughing.

"That shouldn't have upset anybody. How long's he been writing it?"

"Two years."

"On and off, like."

"Between lectures." She smiled at the point he was making, then banged her bottle down on the table. "What a bunch of . . ." She turned to him. "Did you and your wife have fights like this?"

"Not so complex. She used to get fed up sometimes, and then when I got her to say what the problem was, I'd stop doing it, whatever it was, or start. That was about it. She didn't tell me she thought I was a lousy cop, or ask me to quit."

She thought about this, and obviously came to an uncomfortable point in her thinking. "Any word on who killed Timmy Marlow?"

"Not yet." Then he remembered what he wanted to raise with her. "Did he ever come on to you, by the way? I mean, except as you told me, the way he came on to anything in a skirt."

"There's an outdated phrase. No, I was nothing special to him." She laughed. "I don't want to gossip, but the one he was coming on to had enough skirts for all of us. You ever notice that Pat Dakin always wears two or three layers?"

"Pat Dakin? Was he after her? Surely she didn't lower herself . . ." Pickett laughed. "Maybe she thought she was Lady Chatterley?"

"It's a murder inquiry, isn't it, so I'm not gossiping. Yes, he was after her. Should I have told you this before?"

"And when did you say she left here?"

"On Saturday, according to her husband. They had a fight, the Dakins, and she went."

"I'd better have a word with Wilkie, if he hasn't already talked to her."

"Don't run away yet. Tell me what to do about Dennis. Did I go too far?"

Pickett took a swig of beer. "Yeah. I think you did. Telling him the writing he's been doing for the last two years is a pile of crap doesn't leave him much. And maybe you're wrong."

"Maybe. But I'm not wrong about the rest of him."

It's her subject, Pickett thought. She raised it. "You mean the bed part?"

Now she blushed slightly, laughing. "No, no. I was just giving you a sample. If the rest of him was all right, what you call the bed part would be, too. The real problem is that I am no longer enamored of him, not in love with him, so I can now admit to myself that I don't *like* him, and I don't think I ever did. Oh, don't look like that. You don't want me to give you the whole history, do you? Take my word. The point is, now what am I going to do?"

It seemed obvious. "Pack your bags. What's the problem?"

"What about the play? I can't just drive off and leave it."

"Ah. No, you can't. That would finish it. I guess you couldn't ask *him* to leave"

"It's his house."

"So you need somewhere to stay."

"If the Dakins hadn't split up, I could have stayed at their B-and-B and commuted."

"No, you couldn't. I stayed there. You can't even read in bed with the itty-bitty little lamp she gives you. I've got a better idea. Use this." He pointed to the little trailer he had lived in while he was in the early stages of building the cabin. "Until you find a room."

"What a good idea," she said, round-eyed, then gave a little giggle. "Actually, the thought had crossed my mind . . ."

"I know," Pickett said, who had realized it just in time. "I'll show you how it works, then you can move in whenever you like. I warn you, though. Willis will want to visit."

She looked down at the dog. "I think I could stand that."

While Eliza was visiting Pickett, Wilkie and Copps were drinking coffee in Charlotte's café. Copps handed over the list of Marlow's acquaintances he had put together so far, and made a few comments on some of the names.

Wilkie tucked the list away and asked, "Where was Caxton on Friday?"

Copps said quietly, into his wallet, "One thing I learned this morning is that the woman who runs this place is your pal's girlfriend."

"Pickett? So?"

"Isn't he a friend of Caxton's?"

"Don't worry about Pickett," Wilkie said. Then in deference to Copps, to be courteous, he added, "All right. Finish your coffee and we'll talk outside."

In the car, Copps said, "No one mentioned Caxton, being with him or seeing him on Friday. That bother you?"

"I think Marlow was shot by someone he knew, someone he let get too close to him. He said he was going to Toronto, then he turned up in the bush. I think he went up there to meet someone."

"And met up with her husband instead?"

"Possible. You come across anyone likely?"

"No."

"Try this," Wilkie said. "Caxton knew that Marlow had gone to Toronto, right? He would've known that. His girlfriend, Marlow's sister, would have told him. Then some way or another he sees Marlow up near the cottages on Friday. Now, there's been a lot of stuff taken from those cottages lately, so now Caxton knows who's been doing it. So he follows Marlow up the trail. Confronts him, like. Marlow takes him on, and Caxton shoots him. Now he's in a mess. Self-defense will look after the legal side, but what about Marlow's sister? I keep hearing how she doted on her brother. That would be the end of Caxton and Marlow's sister, wouldn't you say?"

"You think that's what happened?"

"No, I just made it up. Anyway, Caxton's gun is the wrong kind."

"You checked, though?"

"I noticed it in his office, in the drawer of his desk, and this morning we got the report of the slug that was found in Marlow's head. It doesn't fit."

"So much for Lyman Caxton."

"I don't know," Wilkie said. "You remember that motel owner who called us right after Marlow's picture came out in the local paper? He called me again this morning to tell me someone was checking up on Marlow's movements. The description was pretty good because he knew he'd have to remember. Caxton. What's he up to?"

"Maybe he's looking for Marlow's killer, like you said he should. Trying to beat us to the finish," Copps said. "And he thinks his girlfriend will be happy if he finds the guy who did her brother."

"That makes more sense than thinking Caxton killed him. But Caxton is playing a little game, all right. We didn't tell him about that motel, and he hasn't told us. He should've, don't you think? And if I didn't already know it, it could be important for me to know that Marlow rented that motel room just for a couple of hours, and yet no one saw a woman. All he did there was shave his beard. Caxton knows that, but he hasn't told me yet." Wilkie paused. "Why the hell did Marlow shave his beard off?"

Copps grinned. "His girlfriend said it tickled. Said if he wanted to go down on her, he'd have to shave it off."

"Or, possibly, he didn't want to be recognized. Anyway, something to think about until we find the killer."

Now Copps delivered his little piece of news. "And what would Caxton be looking for in the bush this morning?" he asked.

"Where?"

"Right around where we found the body. Between there and the river."

"You saw him?"

"He drove past the picnic spot, then went up a little ways and tucked his car out of sight."

"So you followed him?"

"I couldn't do that. There's no place to turn around if he should come back quick, and even if I went in on foot I might never pick him up, so I stayed by that little bridge and waited for him to come out. I figured we could bump into each other and he could tell me what he went in there for. But then I saw him searching the bush around where Marlow was found. You could see him from the bridge. First I thought he was just walking through the bush, then you could see he was going back and forth, looking for something."

"So did you bump into him?"

"No, because I figured he'd tell me he was looking for his car keys. I figured we'd wait until tomorrow at least, see if he says anything to us about it. Then, if he doesn't, ask him. And if he gives some bullshit reason, ask him why he didn't tell us before. 'Cause we might have found whatever it was and not know it was his. You know, if you lose something you tell everyone to watch for it, don't you?"

"Unless it's a gun."

"I thought you might say that." Copps smiled, satisfied.

"Our boys cover the area pretty good?"

"Four guys on their hands and knees all day. They didn't miss anything important."

"Still, Mel Pickett says that Caxton is a bit of an Indian in the bush. I mean, it's just possible he would see something we could miss, being city boys ourselves. Not a gun, no. Something, though. A broken twig, maybe." He glanced across to make sure Copps knew he was joking. "Let's keep an eye on him. Assign someone to watch him. I'll keep him close to me when I can, but let's see where he goes on his own."

CHAPTER 12

When Pickett found the site for his cabin, three years before, he took the precaution of discussing the possibility of a mortgage with the only bank in town, a branch of his own bank in Toronto. He did this not because he could not have managed the deal with his own money, or by taking out a small mortgage on his Toronto house, but because he wanted to make himself known to the manager. He disliked money machines, preferring to withdraw the cash he needed over the counter. He had a credit card, which he hardly ever used except to back up his checks, and when he went on a trip he bought traveler's checks.

Because of this, and because he wanted the status of a valued customer at the Larch River branch, he opened an account there and got to meet the manager, who assured him of his absolute attention at all times should Pickett ever need money or advice. A week later Pickett was in his office raising the question of a mortgage. As he anticipated, the manager said, "No problem," and then began to ask questions and talk about getting head office approval.

Pickett had fully made up his mind to buy the land,

but he didn't trust the owner's evaluation, which he felt was not so much exorbitant as hopeful. The real estate agent who listed the property suggested that Pickett offer a thousand less, which Pickett guessed to be the amount the real estate man and the owner had agreed on when Pickett had appeared on the horizon. The agent also recommended him to a lawyer, a very old man who kept an office over a shoe repair shop in Sweetwater and was familiar with the plot of land Pickett wanted to buy.

"I had a look at it myself," he told Pickett. "I thought it might be something I could use. My nephew wants a place for the summer, and there's nothing left along the river. Geoffrey could have kept a boat at the marina and I thought if he put up a little prefab, an A-frame, maybe, on your piece of land that would be almost as good as having his own place on the river."

"And?"

The lawyer's old face went bland along the seams. "It isn't really suitable for him." He searched his mind for a better reason. "His wife's a bit afraid of the country, you see. She thought it might be lonely."

"Not because the price was too high?"

"It's worth whatever old Moonie can get," Duckett, the lawyer, said.

Pickett knew then he was being asked to pay a large premium, but he didn't mind much; five thousand either way did not make a lot of difference. And yet, as he put it to himself, if he was going to be screwed, he liked to know it was happening, so he asked the bank manager for a mortgage to cover three quarters of the asking price. The manager did not even have to get an independent evaluation but offered in response a loan for half the full price, and agreed, with a little coaxing, that in the opinion of most people in town who had discussed the sale, Pickett was about to be taken by old Moonie.

"You think Moon would have come down?" Pickett asked.

"Put it like that, then, no, I don't. He doesn't need the money, you see. No, he wouldn't."

"Then I wouldn't have got the piece of land I want."

"That's a point," Villiers, the bank manager, said. "That's a point. But it's still my responsibility to tell you the price is too high."

So Villiers did his duty and Pickett sold his Bell Telephone stock for enough money to be able to write a check on his Larch River account for the full cost of the lot, with a sizable sum left in a savings account, where it earned almost no interest at all. As a result, he got a handshake from Villiers whenever he was in the bank, and was accorded a semi-insider status with access to some of the gossip.

On Friday morning, while Pickett was withdrawing some money, Villiers called him into his office, shutting the door behind him. Pickett wondered what he was going to hear, perhaps one of Villiers's filthy, and usually funny, stories. Villiers oiled his business relationships with a stream of very good dirty jokes, a source of wonder to Pickett, who was one of those people who could remember the jokes at his wedding and the one he heard yesterday but nothing in between. This time,

ERIC WRIGHT

though, Villiers had the air of someone wanting to get a worry off his chest. For all his folksy, small-town image, he had created a bond of understanding with Pickett based on their both being big-city boys, really, men who could share a small private amusement at the ways of the Larch River natives. Pickett guessed that he was in for a revelation, the news that the well digger had been apprehended selling his sister to the highway construction crew, perhaps.

Villiers took a bill from a drawer and laid it in front of Pickett. "Look at that," he ordered.

Pickett stared at it. An orange fifty-dollar bill. "Counterfeit?" he asked.

"Turn it over."

In the top left-hand corner were two initials, a B and a C or an O in black ink. Pickett described what he saw.

"Smell it," Villiers ordered.

Pickett checked to see the door was closed, beginning to suspect an elaborate practical joke. He held the bill to his nose and sniffed it warily two or three times.

"Where's it been?" Villiers demanded.

Pickett sniffed it again. "In a barmaid's apron," he tried. "Smells of yeast."

Villiers shook his head. "Flour," he said. "Smells of flour. My girl who brought it to me didn't notice that. But she did notice the initials and she made a connection. She's a smart lass. You know what BC stands for."

"Looks more like BO or BQ."

Villiers said, "BC," and waited.

"Betty Cullen."

"Right. The bill came from the bakery, where Betty

126

put her initials on it when she counted it. She initials all the big bills and the top bill of the stacks of small ones."

"It might have gone to someone else after it left her."

"It did. That's what's so abnormal. Betty runs a small business, takes in a couple of thousand a week. They've had a little safe in their back room since before we opened this branch. They used to deposit in Sweetwater once a week to save driving back and forth every day. We've got a night deposit box here now, so she doesn't need to keep anything overnight. But she said she was used to the weekly deposit, so she carried on with it. Now whenever she gets a fifty or a hundred, she sets it aside for deposit. They're not all that rare, even here, but you don't need them to make change, so the bill should've come straight to us the week she took it in. But it just turned up yesterday. Jenny found it when she was balancing, but she can't remember when she took it in. She only took in four fifties all day, but she recognized this one by the initials when she was counting, so she brought it to me."

"It could've been going the rounds for weeks."

"True enough. But any store round here treats fifties the same as Betty. They don't need them for change."

"Maybe she bought something big at the hardware store or the lumber yard. Paid cash."

"Might've," Villiers agreed immediately, vigorously, not at all inclined to dispute it.

Pickett recognized the response. Villiers was not trying to be fair-minded. Having shared the problem with Pickett, he was now covering himself by agreeing that it might not be a problem at all, retreating behind a show of impartiality, but ready to pop out again either to claim credit or agree that it was utterly innocent, whatever the case turned out to be. Villiers, Pickett suspected, was of Irish descent.

"Did you ask around?"

"I didn't know what to do. It could mean something or nothing. But every time we had a bill before with those initials on, it came straight from Betty. I don't want to ask around."

Pickett saw the point. It was impossible to ask without the risk that it would get back to Betty Cullen, and since the implication might be that her brother had taken it from the till, she might construct a reply to keep her brother's name clean. But Villiers was right to wonder if the bill was significant. Marlow's wallet had been picked clean. The whole town was following the investigation closely, and most of the details that Caxton knew were known to everybody.

"Tell the police."

Villiers looked unhappy. "That's like asking Betty. Isn't it?"

"So why are you asking me?"

"I don't know. You used to be a cop, didn't you? What would you do?"

"I'd tell the OPP. After I'd made sure they understood why I thought it was a bit delicate."

"Would *you*, Mel?"

"Oh shit, all right. I'll tell Sergeant Wilkie, but he might have to go round asking hard questions. You can't be sure he'll be able to keep you out of it."

"Maybe we should forget it."

"You can't do that. Fact is, let's say it, the bill could've come out of Timmy Marlow's wallet, and whoever brought it in could tell the OPP where they got it. It won't have a long trail."

"It'll lead straight here, though, and if it's just Betty paying the plumber cash to get round income tax, GST, stuff like that, she's going to be pissed off with me."

"I'll try and get Wilkie to involve you last." Pickett stood up. "You get a lot of cash trading around here?"

"I'll tell you, Mel. There's always been the usual moonlighting. It's cheaper on one side, and you save the income tax on the other. But people have always felt a little guilty about it. This Goods and Services Tax, though, people hate it. They dodge it as if it's their patriotic duty. There's an electrician near here who reports just enough income to keep his kids in porridge. But his boat and cottage, and his month in Florida—all that is paid for in cash. And the GST isn't a bad tax, the idea of it, anyway. It's just that I think I'm the only person in town who understands it."

CHAPTER 13

Pickett accepted the commission, but instead of having to drive out to Sweetwater he ran into Wilkie leaning into a car window, talking to one of his men outside Caxton's house. "I've got something you might want to know about," Pickett said.

Wilkie straightened up, glanced back at Caxton's house and up and down the street for a place to sit down. "Come for a ride," he said. "I'm parked just down the street."

Pickett joined him in the cruiser and Wilkie pointed the car out of town.

Pickett said, "Why are you watching Caxton?"

"We aren't *watching* him, Mel."

"Bullshit. There's someone sitting near his house day and night. What are you hoping to see? I'll bet I'm the only one who's visited the guy."

"That's right. You are. Fact is, he spends all his time alone or with you. Mostly he just sits looking at the street."

"He's mourning."

"For Marlow?"

"Don't be an asshole. For himself and Betty Cullen."

"Yeah? Well, he's not *doing* anything, for which I'm grateful."

At the junction of the highway he turned away from the direction of Sweetwater. "I've had no lunch," he said. "There's a place up here with the best homemade soup in the county."

"How come you haven't had time to eat? You doing one of these round-the-clock investigations you're always telling the public about? You coulda fooled me."

"Oh, I had time, Mel. I had time. But I made the mistake of going into this ptomaine clinic by the gas station, a real greasy spoon, and you could tell by the broad behind the counter there was no way to trust the food. We just had a coffee . . ."

Pickett was bright red and looking murderous before he realized what Wilkie was up to. "You bastard, " he said. "Who told you?"

"Everybody, Mel. It's that size of town." Wilkie was beside himself with glee. "Shouldn't you be careful, at your age? Rich, randy widower like you. How well do you know her?"

"Knock it off. I remember you now. You always went too goddamn far. Now knock it off."

"Sorry. Sorry. Sorry. Seriously, she looks like a very nice lady. When's the big day?"

"You want to hear what I have to say?"

"Go ahead. I'm just jealous. But I *didn't* have any lunch because Copps was sure she tells you everything she hears."

"He's right. She does. Now listen to me for a minute." Finally he told the tale. He ended, "Villiers, the bank manager, is hoping you might be able to use the information without involving him. He wouldn't want everyone to think their secrets aren't safe with him."

Wilkie said, "All right. So far, one fifty-dollar bill. Could have come from anywhere, and I'll think about it before I have a talk with Marlow's sister. He may have had two or three of them on him. This bank teller—Jenny?—I'll tell the manager to get her to watch out for any more, let us know where they came from. Then I'll ask some more questions." He looked at his watch. "Time for a bowl of soup. This place has got new people running it. The boys say the fish chowder is worth the drive."

Pickett watched the traffic slow down respectfully as the black-and-white cruiser rolled along the highway, down to a responsible hundred kilometers an hour, only ten reasonable kilometers over the limit. Wilkie leaned forward a little, frowned, then shifted into the center passing lane, put on his flasher, and started to overtake the stream of cars. He drove in this way for no more than three minutes, then switched off his flasher and settled in with the stream of traffic, alarming only the drivers in the immediate vicinity. A minute later he pulled off the highway to a small, independent service station with a dining room attached, much like the café Charlotte ran.

The fish chowder was good; so, too, from the comments of the room, were the minestrone, the pea soup, and the chicken-vegetable. When the waitress, a tall, thin woman who was also the cook, had taken their order, Wilkie said, "She's from Toronto, trying to live naturally. All the stuff here is organic or free range. Can you have organic fish?"

"It's not cheap, not like regular soup," Pickett said, reading the small menu.

"That's why it won't last. A few summer cottagers will find it, and they'll use it on their way by, but what about the winter? She won't have too many customers then. People around here aren't used to paying four dollars for a bowl of soup. Have you ever noticed, by the way, the more rural you get, the harder it is to find Ma's old-fashioned cooking? The local people here live on frozen food and pies baked in a factory in Barrie."

"What were you chasing just now?" Pickett asked, more to change the subject than because he cared. He knew Wilkie just enough to know that he was down on all country ways, taking pleasure in pointing out how bad life was in Sweetwater compared with downtown Toronto. He was becoming a little boring on the topic.

"The blue Volvo. Did you see him?"

Pickett searched his memory. "I didn't see anyone do anything wrong."

"I thought it might be a wanted car. I saw it on the bend, just before the road curves round those big rocks, and it had an out-of-province license plate. We had a message yesterday that there was a stolen one believed to be traveling across country, heading east. But that one was from New Brunswick. The stolen one was from Minnesota or Missouri, one of those states in the middle. It's probably in fifty pieces by now in a garage in Montreal."

"You like doing highway patrol?"

"I'm not crazy about parking behind a tree for four hours, but I go for a ride now and then, if that's what you mean. Did you ever do patrol work?"

Pickett shook his head. "I went off the beat straight into Homicide and stayed there until I moved over to Bail and Parole. I did help out with a last little homicide just before I left."

"You live alone now?"

"You saw my cabin. I just have a single bed."

"No, only I was talking to my dad last night on the phone . . ."

"And he told you that I have a granddaughter living with me in Toronto, right?[*] Tell him she's gone back to England, so I'm living alone again. Did he also tell you that she was illegitimate? Or rather, her father was. A wild oat I sowed when I was with the air force in England at the end of the war. She came looking for me a while ago, and I gave her a place to stay. She's gone now, though, back to university. She might come back one day. I hope so. He tell you all that, your dad, did he?"

Wilkie looked for another topic. "Would you think of marrying again?" he asked eventually.

"What is it you really want to know? Ask me. I'll tell you."

Wilkie colored but said nothing.

"You're being goddamn personal, you know that?" Pickett continued. "Like one of those morning TV hosts thinks he can ask any question he likes, because they're

[*] See *A Sensitive Case*.

careful to get only the kind of people on the show who wouldn't tell him to fuck off. I don't know you that well to talk about my private life."

"I just wondered."

"I know."

Later, after he had taken Pickett home, Wilkie examined his question from all angles and decided that it was a perfectly ordinary, reasonable query, and that Pickett had not been entitled to give him a bad time over it. Wilkie had meant it in a general, theoretical sort of way, but Pickett had taken it as a particular inquiry. Which meant, Wilkie concluded, that Pickett was thinking of marrying again, and he was embarrassed about it.

Wilkie had the happy idea of approaching Caxton privately about the fifty-dollar bill, on the assumption that he might know something about the way Marlow's sister conducted her business and her relationship with her brother that would make the information trivial, so he wouldn't have to approach Betty Cullen.

"It was handed over the counter at the bank," Wilkie said. "You see the problem? It could mean something. If Betty initialed it, that would usually mean that she planned to deposit it, wouldn't it? So what could have happened? The only possibility that interests me is that she gave it to Timmy herself, and it was in his wallet when he was killed."

"Tax dodge," Caxton said, promptly. "She could've given that to almost anyone. Always cheaper to pay in cash." He turned away to keep his distance from Wilkie, then said, almost over his shoulder, "That isn't like her, though. It might've come out of Timmy's wallet, but Betty wouldn't necessarily know about it. I caught him once with his hand in the till." He added, "No good asking Betty. When I told her what I'd seen, she even told *me* that she had told Timmy to take the money. Defending him, she was. And she will still. She won't want anyone to think her little brother was a thief. No, you won't get anything out of her. I see where you're heading: you think that if you could find out where the bill came from you'd have a line on the killer. I doubt it. I'll give you odds that if you do trace it you'll find it was used to buy gas, up on the highway, something like that."

"I think I'm going to have to talk to her myself," Wilkie said. "How is she?"

"I haven't seen her. Haven't you heard? She's leaving. She still hasn't reopened the shop. She's leaving. Me and her have broken up."

"Why is that?"

"It has to do with the fact that someone shot her brother. Any more stupid fucking questions?"

Wilkie waited for a minute until Caxton stopped glaring at him. "She still there now?"

"Didn't you hear? *I don't know. I don't fucking know. I haven't seen her. We ain't speaking.*"

Wilkie let him walk away, then turned to cross the street to the bakery.

It took a long time for Betty Cullen to open the door. Wilkie had to knock hard twice, and then step back so that he could be seen from behind the curtain of an upstairs window.

At last her voice came through the door. "Yes?"

"OPP. Can I come in?"

She let him in and rehooked the chain, then led him into the sitting room. He showed her the bill without saying anything, and she turned it over and over. "That's my initial," she said at last. She handed it back to him. "You found that in Timmy's wallet, I suppose. I gave it to him for spending money. I forget how much I gave him. Two hundred."

"How many fifties?"

"I can't remember. How many did you find?"

"Could you have given one to someone for a job they'd done for you? Someone who wanted cash."

She thought about that for a while, then shook her head. "I'd never do that. Everyone around here knows that I would never do that. The government could check up on you. But I could give money to Timmy if I liked, couldn't I?"

But as Wilkie understood it, Betty initialed money that was already made up for deposit, not the bills she slipped to her brother.

CHAPTER 14

Then, three days later, another fifty-dollar bill with Betty Cullen's initials appeared, this time in Sweetwater. The banks there had been alerted by the OPP to watch for marked bills, and one of the clothing stores had included the bill in its regular deposit. The store could not identify the customer who had passed it, but the owner had the bright idea of checking the cash register, which was modern enough to indicate on the sales receipt how much money had been tendered for each transaction, in order to calculate and announce the proper change. There had been fifty dollars offered for an item of thirty-two dollars, which meant it must have been a single bill. The item was a pair of work boots, being offered on sale.

"Those are the bright yellow kind," Wilkie said. "Should be easy to spot."

But the assumption that anyone seen in Larch River wearing new yellow work boots might be a killer was very shaky. The bill that had turned up in the Sweetwater clothing store probably had come from a local carpenter, who had got it from someone else. Or a hundred other possibilities. Nevertheless Wilkie brought in half a dozen extra men to help take a casual look at as many of the boots in Larch River as they could manage. They had to be careful; cross-questioning the local citizenry about their boots would surely send a warning signal through the town very quickly; it would be a slightly absurd and therefore memorable inquiry, to be passed on, grinning, to everyone before the police got all the way round. So they split up and went from workplace to workplace, pretending to be looking for strangers.

The excuse that Wilkie invented came to him when he learned that the stolen Volvo had been found abandoned near Huntsville, where the thief had apparently run out of gas, and all units of the OPP had been asked to keep an eye out for hitchhikers. Someone claimed to have seen the driver leave the car, so Wilkie had a rough description, so vague that he simply lifted an old sketch from another file, one that corresponded to the description, and made a dozen copies. The police now began a methodical check of every house and workplace in Larch River, looking for someone wearing a new pair of yellow boots.

They found three. Two of them, a worker in the lumber mill and a man who sold wood-burning stoves, were known to Caxton and very unlikely suspects. A third, though, was suggested by Caxton himself. "Try Siggy Siggurdson," he said. "He had new boots on last week, but I didn't think nothing about it. Not then."

"Is he likely? What do you know about him?"

"He calls himself a guide, but most of the time he's on welfare. There's a guy named Ramsey who owns a little tourist lodge upriver. If any of his guests wants to go fishing, he or his son takes them out, but if he has several people who want to fish at the same time, he gets Siggy to help out. He uses Siggy just enough so that with a few weeks' work when the lumberyard is busy, Siggy qualifies for unemployment insurance all winter. Mainly he sponges off his mother. From time to time she gets sick of him hanging around and kicks him out, but he's generally back a day or so later. She takes the attitude that everyone's got it in for her boy, until he steals something off her to buy himself a bottle, then she lays a complaint, which I tear up a couple of days later when she feels sorry for him again."

"Let's go see him."

"You mind if I stay here?"

Wilkie waited for an explanation.

Caxton said, "Siggy isn't very popular around here, but I'd as soon not be there when you arrest him for murder. I have to live here afterward. And if you're wrong he's gonna think that I put you up to it." He stood up abruptly. "Oh, shit, he's gonna know that, anyway. Let's go."

"Found your chain saw," Caxton said later, over a beer on Pickett's porch. "Under Siggy's bed, where I figured in the first place."

"You got it with you?"

"Wilkie took it. Needs it for evidence."

"You sure it's mine?"

"Brand-new Husqvarna with a little nick in the handle."

"Won't be brand-new now, not after two years."

140

"Siggy never used it. Too scared to use it or sell it. I made a point two years ago of scaring the shit out of him, so he never brought it out, and he never stole from you again." He paused. "I knew he was a thief, but this latest . . . I wouldn't have guessed it in a million years."

"No?"

"No. He's a tub of lard. If he'd done anything like that, I would've guessed he'd've been in my office every day with suggestions, showing what a good citizen he is."

"He's got a new pair of yellow boots, paid for with a marked fifty," Pickett said, grinning. "It's a start, Lyman."

"Looks pretty good, doesn't it?"

Pickett thought Caxton seemed a little excited by the news, an excitement he was trying not to show. It was probably relief, Pickett thought. If Timmy's killer had been found, then Caxton might still be able to persuade Betty to stay, especially if it was Siggy. From Caxton's point of view, Siggy was the ideal killer.

"He started with the usual bluster," Caxton continued. "Said the money was a tip from some American he'd guided earlier in the summer. Wilkie offered to contact all the Americans he had guided this summer to confirm it—Ramsey, the camp owner, would have a list—then Siggy backed off, said that he really meant that he'd made change for someone else who'd been given the fifty while he was working as a guide. When we threatened to check this out, Siggy said he was just someone he met in a beer parlor, didn't know his name. There he stuck. He liked that story. So we accepted that and just moved on to ask him what he was doing on the trail on Friday, implying someone like me had seen him. Siggy had already told so many lies he was in a hell of a tangle, so he said he'd gone up there to check on some smoke. He was just passing, he said, and saw some smoke, and then he gave us a big bunch of bull-shit about city people not realizing how dangerous campfires were at this time of year with the fire hazard so high. But we had him now: he'd admitted being in the area when Marlow was killed and he had passed a fifty that must have come from Marlow."

"Has he been charged?"

"Not yet. They took him back to Sweetwater to get a search warrant."

"To look for the gun."

Caxton nodded. "I doubt if we'll find it. Siggy's too cute for that."

"Let me know what happens."

When Wilkie returned with a warrant and searched Sig-gurdson's house, he cleared up another of the local mys-teries. In the middle of the woodpile, buried deep enough so that his mother could deny knowledge of its existence, they found much of the stuff that had lately been reported stolen from the cottages. And under Sig-gurdson's mattress, there were two more fifty-dollar bills. So they charged him with theft and waited for him to confess. They didn't find the gun or any more money.

Siggy tried for a better reason for being on the trail than the one he had offered before.

Caxton continued the story. "Now we had the stuff

from his woodpile, he said that that's what he was after. After the cottagers were all gone he figured he'd take a little look around, see what there was to be picked up. He knew he wouldn't bump into me, he said, because he'd seen me working in my office, through the window. When Siggy tells us what really happened on that trail, we'll start all over again."

And that was how it happened. Wilkie sent all of Siggy's clothes to the forensic laboratory, explaining to Siggy that if there was a single trace from Marlow on his clothes the lab would find it. One of Marlow's hairs would make it very easy. Then Siggy told them what had happened.

This time Wilkie told the story. "He claims he found Marlow dead on the trail on Friday night. He'd gone up there, like he said, to see if there was anything left worth picking up, and stumbled over Marlow's body. He practically fell over Timmy in the dark, he said."

"Was he long dead?" Pickett asked.

"Siggy said he wasn't stiff. Said he tried to see if there was any sign of life, but he couldn't find any. Said he'd been shot in the face, but we knew that."

"So he robbed him."

"He said the wallet was on the ground nearby. Yeah, he took the money and left him there. That fits. Siggy figured that would make it look like some casual killer shot Marlow for his money."

"Then he rolled Marlow into the gully?"

"He says not. Says he just took off. Someone else did that, he says. He'd be bound to, of course. He's trying to give off this picture of an impulsive act he's sorry for.

Dumping his old friend in the gully is pretty cold-blooded."

Pickett said, "It's not bad, is it? I mean, he confesses to a bunch of robberies, and to robbing a body, but it's going to be hard to shake him into anything more. Does he have a reputation as a roughhouser?"

"He's a jerk-off. A slimy bag of pus. You ever see a movie called *Beau Geste*? The old one? There's a guy in that who plays a kind of suck to the Foreign Legion sergeant. That's Siggurdson. Caxton says he's capable of anything that doesn't involve pain to himself. If you found him with a gun you could be pretty sure he'd stolen it and was looking to sell it. Caxton says there's no way he'd go up against Marlow with or without a gun. I don't know what the hell happened up on that trail, but if he did kill Marlow, then it was an accident, and he panicked. He couldn't get drunk enough to find the guts to set it up. I told Brendan to keep suggesting to Siggy that it was an accident. Manslaughter."

Pickett said, "How did he know it was Marlow in the dark? From the wallet?"

Wilkie looked startled at the idea, then relaxed. "Siggy knew who it was, all right." He paused to think. "See, Marlow hadn't been mauled yet. The animals hadn't got to him. Siggy knew the guy well, see. Oh yeah." There was satisfaction in Wilkie's voice. He was not reassuring himself, but putting every comma into place.

"Charge him yet?"

"Siggy's changed his story so many times I'm waiting for the confession. Or maybe we'll sweat it out of him.

In the meantime we've got him on seven counts of robbery and one of desecrating a body. We're turning over his place again, see if we can find the gun." Wilkie was thinking of something as he spoke. "Siggy gave us someone else to talk to, though. Kind of while we're waiting for him to break down." Wilkie laughed. "You remember that Marlow used to shack up with Linda McCourt, in the school-teacher's cottage round the point? Someone interrupted them one afternoon. Siggy says that he knows who interrupted them. Pat Dakin, the schoolteacher's wife."

"Siggy get all this on video? He sounds like a real slimebag. I wouldn't trust a word he says."

"He claims he saw her. He says he saw her approach the cabin, then back off. Her own cabin. Must have been confusing for her, Siggy says, because Siggy knew that in his spare time Marlow was humping Pat Dakin, too. On the weekends."

"She used the cottage on weekends to *write*. So Marlow probably did her a good turn, fixed the generator or something. Siggy's mind did the rest. A lot of people must have known that Marlow was after her. Even Eliza knew. He used to go to their play practice when the Dakin woman was still in the play." Pickett held no brief for Marlow's morals, and he disliked what he knew of Pat Dakin, but the two of them seemed like fine, upstanding citizens compared with what he had already heard about Siggurdson.

Wilkie thought about this and shook his head. "Siggy didn't make it up. He watched them through the window."

"Why's he talking about it?"

"He's offering her up to us. Maybe she did it, he says. He doesn't know why she would but we have to ask. The thing is, if she was up to the cottage during the week and surprised her boyfriend diddling someone else, in her cottage yet, might she have gotten unhappy enough to shoot him?"

"You think so?"

"No, but we have to try every possibility. Until Siggy gives in."

"Seems to me another possibility is that Siggurdson was trying to blackmail Marlow. Sounds to me like Siggurdson spent time watching people, you know, a voyeur. We used to call them Peeping Toms."

Wilkie shook his head. "You think Marlow would have cared? The idea of someone like John Dakin coming after him wouldn't bother him. He'd laugh at him. He might not like the idea of Siggurdson watching him, though, but I would guess his reaction to that would have been to kick Siggurdson's teeth in, not pay him bribe money."

"How about Linda McCourt?"

"That would have worried Marlow a bit, I would think. Old McCourt looks like a rough bugger. I'll talk to Caxton about it."

CHAPTER 15

As the police continued to hold Siggurdson, and the town learned something of the evidence against him, they accepted what they heard, and agreed that he was the person most likely to have done it.

Charlotte said, "Nobody liked Timmy Marlow, and they aren't that sorry he's dead, though they don't say so, out of respect for Betty. In the beginning, everyone was saying that Timmy had come up against a husband finally, and they hoped the husband would get away with it. Some people said maybe it was the woman herself, and they've been trying to think of a woman around here who knows about guns. I don't know of any. This isn't Texas, or even Alberta."

But when it was learned that the police were questioning Pat Dakin, all other theories were abandoned in her favor. From the Larch River point of view, she was a good choice as suspect because she, too, was not much liked because of her perceived snobbishness, and the fact that she bought all her groceries in Sweetwater instead of at the Larch River IGA. Opinion had it that she deserved what she got. It was irritating to realize that she had not snubbed Marlow as she had almost everybody else in town, but there was some satisfaction in the knowledge that it had ended badly for the pair of them. As for Siggy, someone suggested that he had probably seen Marlow going up the trail, knew that Pat Dakin was at home, and followed Marlow to watch.

Wilkie took Caxton with him to Toronto to question Pat Dakin. "Just listen for any little discrepancies," he said. "Don't get into the act."

They found her in a small house on Atlas Avenue, on the edge of the old Italian district. She explained, as she let them in, holding the door against a large orange-colored dog, "I'm dog-sitting. I needed somewhere to live and these people have gone to Europe for a month, so they've let me have the house rather than put Honey in a kennel. He's still only a puppy. Down, Honey. Down. Down. *Down. Sit*, for Christ's sake! Sit! Sit! Sit! Sit! Sit!"

Caxton leaned over the dog, said, "Sit," and touched his hindquarters. Honey quivered and sat. Caxton said, "Stay," and the dog lay down.

Pat Dakin said, "That's incredible. He won't do a thing for me."

"He'll be all right."

Wilkie said, "You probably know we're here to find out if you know anything that will help us to investigate the death of Tim Marlow."

Her response was noisy and dramatic. "I know nothing about this Marlow person. He came to the odd rehearsal and his name got linked to mine because he told people he found me . . . attractive, I suppose. Nothing to do with me." She waved an arm as if to brush Marlow away.

Wilkie looked through his notebook. "We have a witness who was watching through the window of your cabin three weeks ago, on a Saturday afternoon, about four o'clock. He's prepared to swear to what he saw. And in your original statement you said you spent this Friday night in your cottage. Our witness said you didn't."

The dog jumped up at some misunderstood signal and tried to mount Pat Dakin's leg.

"He keeps doing this," she said, dropping her pose. "Stop it. Stop it!" She tried to push him off. Encouraged, Honey humped faster.

Caxton said, "Put your hand around his nose, tight, squeeze it hard, and say, 'Down.' "

She did as she was told, and Honey quieted immediately and lay at her feet, panting.

Pat Dakin said, "Why does he find me . . . attractive?"

Caxton said, "He doesn't. At that age, dogs'll try and jump Santa Claus. Nothing to do with if you're attractive."

All three of them looked at Honey for a few moments before Wilkie returned to his question. The interruption had given Dakin a chance to decide on her response.

"All right. I *was* having an affair with Tim," she said, "odd as that may seem." She stared hard at the dog. "We were to spend the weekend in a tourist lodge in Tralee, about forty miles north of Larch River. I have the registration receipt in my purse. He never turned up and I came back to Larch River on Saturday morning, only to formally leave my husband. That is the extent of my part in this affair."

"Didn't you look for him in Larch River?"

"Where? I did look in the bakery. He wasn't there. I'd been dumped. He'd done it to me before, and I decided he wasn't going to do it again."

Wilkie asked her, routinely, if she was aware of any of Marlow's enemies, but she insisted she knew nothing about him. So for the moment, Wilkie was satisfied to locate her forty miles from the murder, and asked only that if anything occurred to her that might help them, she should get in touch.

Outside, he asked Caxton, "Where'd you learn about dogs?"

"I grew up with them. They're animals. Unless they've got rabies, they behave for a reason." Caxton looked into the distance. "She wasn't much help, was she?"

For some time now Pickett had been thinking of out-buildings, not in any grand sense but in the sense that he needed a woodshed and a place to keep the snow off his car, and maybe a toolshed. Nothing elaborate, because he had passed the point where he wanted to lift heavy logs again, to risk a strained back, a hernia, or the broken ankle that comes from stumbling over a log late in the day.

There would have been no difficulty about slapping together a few simple structures made of two-by-fours and plywood; decently clad in cedar siding they would not be eyesores. But Pickett was proud of his cabin and wanted any additions to conform to it in appearance, so he waited until a simple solution to the problem of out-buildings and the energy to carry out such a solution presented themselves.

Then, after the hydro had been connected, he was visited by Stan Nykoruk, a man who serviced outboard motors and small gasoline engines, to see if he wanted to sell the little generator that he had built the cabin with. But building the cabin had induced a pleasure in being self-sufficient in Pickett, and he decided to keep the generator in case of a major storm that would bring down the power lines, when he would be glad to be able to hook up the generator again. He didn't actually say this to Nykoruk, because the mechanic might have pointed out that a woodstove and a handful of candles were all he needed to get him through most emergencies, and then Pickett might have had to agree that the generator was in fact not a useful piece of backup equipment but an object of sentiment, roughly the equivalent of the ax his great-grandfather used to build *his* cabin.

What he actually told Nykoruk was that it was spoken for already, but he gave him a beer so his trip wouldn't be wasted, and took him on a tour of the place.

When Pickett explained his next project, Nykoruk said, "You should take that old shed of Harlan's off his hands. He's been trying to get the boys down at the Sweetwater firehall to burn it down. You know it? On the concession road up above the river. Harlan owns a farm there, derelict. He's been waiting for a developer to come along and give him his price."

"Whereabouts, exactly?"

"I'll take you. Got a minute?"

They climbed into Nykoruk's pickup and drove

151

through the town to the bridge over the river, then back two miles south to a concession road. There they turned back in the direction of the town and drove to a place where seven or eight abandoned buildings stood on a piece of land that had reverted to scrub. Pickett had seen the farm before when he first explored the area, but had not remembered the buildings. Now he saw that one of them might provide exactly the material he needed. It was not a barn; it was too small for that. On the other hand it was more than a shed. Probably some kind of storage space for farm implements, harrows and seeders and such. Pickett thought if it really was derelict, then the owner might let him take away some of the ancient silver-gray planking, which would merge perfectly with his cabin. He looked at the building from the fence, making a rough guess that all he needed was the planking from two sides.

"Who's Harlan?" he asked Nykoruk.

"Percy Harlan. He owns the motel and the gas station and nearly everything else around here."

Then Pickett remembered the name. Charlotte's boss. He had long ago heard that he was the town's leading entrepreneur. As well as the gas station, the motel, and the coffee shop, he owned the grocery store, the marina, the two schoolbuses, and the only taxi license in the town. He lived in one of the units in his own motel, but it was widely known that during the busy summer season he rented out his own unit and slept on a cot in the office.

Pickett said, "If I can get it off him, would you give me a hand to take it down?"

Nykoruk looked doubtful, and Pickett offered a sacrifice. "For the generator?"

"Me and the truck for a day," Nykoruk offered, after some thought.

"That should do it."

Nykoruk drove him back to his own car, and Pickett went in search of Harlan, first stopping in at the café to talk to Charlotte.

"He was planning to have them burn it down at the next town picnic," she confirmed. "It's become a risk, see. I understand even if someone was trespassing and it fell in on them, he could be sued. Lot of those planks are pretty loose. But if the fire department burned it, he wouldn't have to pay to have it pulled down."

"Where can I find him?"

"He's in and out all the time. I'll call you when he gets back."

He drove home and waited. The phone rang within the hour.

When he arrived at the coffee shop, Charlotte pointed to a door at the end of the dining room. "He's in there."

Harlan's "office" was a storage room. Pickett knew from Charlotte that local people came to Harlan as to a pawnbroker. He would buy anything, if it was cheap enough, and keep it for years, if necessary, until someone needed it. There was at least twice as much furniture as the room needed: two desks, several office chairs, some filing cabinets, as well as three television sets and a lot of electronic equipment. Harlan worked from a desk covered in papers, and behind him, along the wall, a long row of bulldog grips held more paper. He was at least seventy years old, with the appearance of someone who would be a dandy if he could afford it. His hair was thin, though still black, and parted in the center. He wore a shabby suit, with a neat but slightly greasy bow tie. His nails were manicured, and he had the habit of splaying them often in front of him on the desk, examining them for flaws. If Pickett had not known that he was almost certainly a millionaire, he would have admired the brave way in which an obviously impoverished man was keeping up appearances. Harlan pointed to a chair. "Pull that up to the desk, Mel," he said. "Charlotte says you want me to give you that shed of mine." He laughed. "That's what she *said*." He shook his head. "I've hung on to that shed for a long time, Mel. A long time. I could have sold it a dozen times, but I don't want that lumber to be misused. It's rare. That's what it is. Rare."

"I heard you were going to burn it down."

Harlan jumped, as if from a small electrical shock. "Burn it? *Burn it?* You know what that lumber is worth in the city? Some of those interior decorators would pay ten dollars a foot."

"Delivered? That's just about what it would cost you to ship it to them. I'll take it away for nothing. Some of it."

Harlan laughed. "Can't do that, Mel. It is Mel, isn't it? No, I couldn't do that. Got to be fair to myself. Tell you what. Let's take a run out there now, take a look. Then we'll know what we're talking about."

Harlan guided them by a slightly different route, along a farm road full of potholes.

"Where does this road come out."

"Nowhere. Or rather, it comes out here. It's just a service road. It leads into the other concession road that runs into town."

"That's the one I was on before."

They pulled up by the shed and looked at it from the car. "I'll take it off your hands before it gets you into trouble." Pickett offered.

Harlan laughed. "Sure." He looked the shed over. Some of the boards were already drooping from a single nail and there were several gaps in the roof. "Come on. What'll you give me for it?"

Pickett shook his head, repeating what Charlotte had told him. "That place isn't safe. You realize that if one of those roof timbers fell on someone, you'd be responsible. If I were you, I'd burn it down, quick."

Harlan smiled. "Never mind my problems. How many planks you need?"

"I'd like two walls. That'd do me."

"Tell you what. Now you've told me about the terrible risks I'm running, I won't be able to sleep. You find someone to dismantle the whole place, at your risk, mind, and you can have two walls as your fee. How's that? And the rest has to be neatly stacked."

Pickett was fairly sure that Nykoruk could take this shed down in a day, with his help. "It's a deal."

They left the car and Harlan led the way around to the end of the shed, where the double doors stood wide open. Harlan scratched his head and walked inside.

"Careful," he said. "Somebody's been sleeping in my bed, looks like."

Inside the empty shed was a late-model car with just enough dust and bird droppings to show it had been there for a few days.

"Leave it alone," Pickett said immediately, as Harlan went to open a door.

Harlan said, "It's one of the cottagers, getting free parking."

"I don't think so," Pickett said.

"You think it's connected with the fella who got shot?"

"I think it's likely. Close the doors. I'll phone Wilkie."

The car, it turned out, had been rented from an agency in Dumpy Lake. It had been signed out to a man in Jacob's Creek. When they checked on the driver, he told them that he had not rented the car, but that the identification was his, taken from a wallet stolen from him some weeks before. When Wilkie searched the car he found a sports bag in the trunk with a label identifying it as the property of T. Marlow of Larch River.

"You still think Siggurdson did it?" Pickett asked Wilkie.

"That's who I've got in the cells," Wilkie said.

"Even without the bag in the trunk, there's got to be more to it than that. A stranger wouldn't know about that shed. Would Marlow steal a car to meet Siggurdson?"

"So what do we think now? Marlow went to Dumpy

Lake and shaved his beard off to match the false ID, which, by the way, he probably bought off Siggy. Clean-shaven, he looks a bit more like the picture. Okay?" Wilkie thought for a while. "Then he drove back here and holed up in the bush, waiting for his rendezvous. Did he smoke? We've got clear signs that someone was sitting in ambush up there—the guy left some cigarette butts behind. Store-bought by the way, which is another little mystery, though I think Siggy might clear it up if he was inclined." He started again. "So Marlow rents a car, drives up here . . ." But now Wilkie had run out of ideas.

"You think he shaved just to fit the picture on the ID?"

"Why else?"

Pickett offered him a fragment of Caxton's theory. "Could be he didn't want to be recognized as he drove through town."

"We don't know, do we? It'll all come clear soon, I wouldn't doubt."

"It's a lot of trouble just to kill Siggurdson."

"You think so?" Wilkie had had time to think. "If Siggy was found dead, then one of the people we'd want to talk to would be Marlow, right? So Marlow put together this fancy alibi. But Siggy might have been waiting for Marlow to try something like that. I think it holds together. I think I know what I'm doing."

Siggurdson was charged with manslaughter the next day. Wilkie had what he considered a partial confession in Siggurdson's admission that he had robbed the body;

it was easy enough to construct a motive of blackmail, based on Siggurdson's admission that he had watched Marlow and Pat Dakin having sex. The gun was missing, but it was obviously at the bottom of a gully somewhere in the bush. They had enough of a case to proceed to trial.

Siggurdson, of course, had no money for lawyers, and was appointed a legal aid defender. When Pickett heard that Siggurdson had been charged, he accepted that Wilkie knew what he was doing and forgot about it. It was difficult, anyway, to sympathize with a Siggy, a Peeping Tom who robbed the body of his dead crony, and easy to believe he had done the ultimate deed.

Besides, Pickett was more concerned with his own problems, specifically with his relationship with Charlotte, which now had to move forward or go back. Winter was coming and with it the assumption that he would close up the cabin and return to Toronto until April. But Larch River was Charlotte's home. Could he drive up every Sunday all winter just for dinner, etc.? Would she let him? Would she want him to? As far as Larch River was concerned, it would be a declaration of sorts, and the world would wait for the next step, or announcement. Was Charlotte, even now, waiting?

At their age, such a step seemed to require more guarantees than it used to. The young could get blithely spliced for life in the hope that it might work, but he, and presumably Charlotte, had experienced and could foresee all the bumps in the road ahead.

Give her up, then. He tried that one in his head and rejected it immediately, absolutely refusing to take responsibility for making himself unhappy. So he would ask her. But there were real consequences. Where would they live? Between them they had three homes, counting the cabin. Which would they retain? He didn't want to live in Toronto on his own, but he didn't want to spend twelve months of the year in Larch River, either. They ought to settle these questions first. If they turned out to be insuperable, then that would have been the test. They shouldn't get hitched.

Back and forth he went, making little progress, until it was almost a relief to find Mrs. Siggurdson on his doorstep, asking for help.

THREE

He watched her walk up the track from the gravel road at the end of his lot: a huge, dirty-looking woman in elephantine black pants, a greasy blue-and-gray man's windbreaker, and a beret jammed on her head, holding some of her lank black hair off her face. On her feet were a pair of old running shoes. Pickett wondered where she had walked from. There had been no sound of a car, so she must have traveled at least the mile from town on foot. As she approached he saw that her cheeks and nose were covered in bright red veins. She seemed to be about sixty, but it was hard to tell, so weathered and dirty was her face.

He stood back from the window and watched her climb the steps up to the porch and bang on the door. He guessed she was a beggar of some sort, perhaps a rural bum, a derelict. He opened the door, wondering what to give her that would satisfy his desire to be charitable but would not have her coming back repeatedly. A sandwich, maybe, and a cup of coffee.

She looked at the piece of paper in her hand. "This the Pickett place?"

He liked the sound of that. "The Pickett place" made

it seem like a landmark, as if he belonged here. "I'm Mel Pickett," he said.

She looked at him, waiting, as if she had done her share. It was his move. Then, "You don't know me."

But now he did have a faint memory of her, seen occasionally in the town. She was some kind of neighbor, then, needing help. "I've seen you around, I think."

"I ain't seen you that I know of. I'm Evie Siggurdson."

At first he leaped to the absurd assumption that she was Siggurdson's wife, but she was surely twenty years too old for that. And then he remembered Caxton saying that Siggurdson lived with his mother.

It was time to let her in. He picked up Willis, who was watching her warily, and stepped back. At first she stood just inside the doorway, until Pickett pushed a chair in place, and she sat down on the edge, looking round at the cabin. Pickett sat opposite her.

"Fixed up nice," she said appraisingly. "You bin here a couple of years, Siggy says. Never came around before."

Didn't Siggy have a first name, he wondered, not even to his mother? Pickett realized that she was probably trying to be sociable, but did not have the habit or the vocabulary to manage routine courtesies. "What's the problem?" he asked when she lapsed back into silence.

"You're a copper," she said.

"I was."

"You bin involved with my Siggy."

"Not involved. I know what's been happening. I heard about it. It's the OPP and Lyman Caxton you want."

"I don't want that cocksucker. He's in with that bitch in the bake shop. I went to the bakeshop but she wouldn't talk to me. Wouldn't open the door. Fella in the beer parlor said you was friends to the OPP."

"I know them."

"Tell them Siggy didn't do it. They'd listen to youse."

"I doubt it. Why should they?"

"I'm telling youse. My Siggy din't shoot Timmy Marlow. They're just arrestin' him to save trouble. Same with that lawyer they got."

Now Pickett took the first step. "They've got a lot of evidence against him."

"He din't do it. They made it up."

"What do you have to go on?"

"He told me he din't do it. I know Siggy. He din't do it. They bin on at him steady since they picked him up. Soon he'll git tired and tell 'em anything they want. And that lawyer they got for him, he'll put him up to it. He's on their side."

Pickett felt a small breath of apprehension. Like everyone familiar with the legal system, he knew enough lawyers who made a nice living from legal aid by getting their clients to plead guilty to a reduced charge. Plea bargaining. It saved a lot of trouble for both sides and enabled the lawyer to take a much bigger caseload. Some of these lawyers were known in the trade as "dump trucks" because they hauled away all the detritus of the legal system that nobody else wanted to deal with. Pickett knew of several in Toronto. What she seemed to be saying was that they had found one for her son. But then, she would be bound to regard any lawyer, including the local civil rights lawyer, who advised her son to plead guilty, as working for the police.

"What's his name, this lawyer?"

"I don't know."

He could find out. "You want a cup of coffee? Or a beer?"

She looked at him as if it was a tricky choice, even a test he was setting her. "I'll take a beer," she said, finally.

He looked at his watch. "It's nearly lunchtime. Want a sandwich?"

She nodded immediately and unzipped her windbreaker.

Pickett found enough liverwurst for two sandwiches, gave her one, and poured them each a beer. She sniffed the sandwich, took a bite, and filled up her mouth with beer and mixed it all together. She had only three teeth and seemed to chew with the back of her throat, keeping her mouth open. Small pieces of the sandwich tumbled over her lips and onto her bosom.

Pickett watched, fascinated. He did not think he had ever seen anyone so dirty in his life, apart from street people. All the seams and veins of her hands, the creases of her face and neck, were blackened as if marked with crayon, all except, now, the moist area around her mouth, which became clean when she wiped her sleeve over it. And now he caught the smell of her and made an excuse of getting some paper towels from the kitchen, returning to open the door, commenting on the fine day, and shifting his chair to the side and back.

When she had eaten the sandwich and drunk most of the beer, Pickett said, "I don't think I can do anything."

He tried to think of some advice, but the only suggestions he could think of, like hiring another lawyer, or, if she thought it was worthwhile, getting a detective, were useless. She didn't have the money to create a real response to the charges against Siggy.

"Seems like nobody can," she said. Her face twitched and quivered as if from a toothache and Pickett realized that she was in the distress that made other women cry. He hoped this wouldn't happen to her.

"Let's go over it," he said. "Siggy—what's his first name, by the way?"

"Ulro. Nobody calls him that, though. Not even me. He don't like it."

"All right. Way I heard it was that after Siggy realized that he might be in big trouble, then he admitted he stumbled over Marlow's body and robbed it. That's enough for a couple of years, right there. He says he didn't kill Marlow, but there's no evidence that anyone else was around that night. Fact is, someone shot Marlow just about the time Siggy says he robbed him. You can't blame the OPP for seeing it different."

"Siggy didn't ever own a gun."

"They haven't found the weapon yet. See, even if it was Marlow's gun and they had a struggle and Siggy got the gun and it went off accidentally, then Siggy should have come back and told the police."

"He would've, if that's what'd happened. My Siggy's a fuck-up, but he wouldn't take on Timmy Marlow."

"Not even if he thought Marlow was going to kill him?"

"Siggy's no good in a fight."

Pickett tried another route. "Did he ask you to come to me?"

"I told you. He's about whipped. He just says he din't kill him, and that's all he says except not to worry. But I don't want him to go to the penitentiary. He coo'n't handle that." Once again she seemed about to cry.

Pickett got up and opened another beer for her. "What do you think I can do?"

"You're in with those guys. You see if you think my Siggy done it. If he din't, tell them."

Be a friend at court.

"I couldn't pay you much," she said. "Maybe a little at a time. Afterward."

Pickett thought, You don't have a choice, because she doesn't, either. "Okay. I doubt if I can do anything, but I won't charge you for trying." After all, old teachers helped out at literacy centers. Maybe this was something old cops could do. "I'll do it like you say. I'll ask them, and if I don't think Siggy did it, I'll tell them, and tell you, too. You take it from there." He tried to think of some way of communicating that what he was undertaking was only a futile gesture, because he could see from the relaxation in her stance that she had got what she came for; her troubles were over. But he was doing it because he had never met anyone less likely to generate the sympathy of his fellow beings than Siggy, from what he'd heard of him, or his mother; for that reason he felt sorry for her. No one should be that destitute of support.

He couldn't say any of this to Mrs. Siggurdson. "I have to tell you, though, that right now it looks bad."

"You think he done it?" She stiffened slightly.

"At this stage, it looks likely."

"He din't do it."

"I'll ask the police, see if I can find out what the case is like. They probably won't tell me."

"Sure, they will. You're in with them. When can I come back?"

"Oh no. No. I'll ask and I'll make up my mind, and then I'll come and find you. Where do you live?"

She gave him directions to the Siggurdson place, a house on a concession road, a home that Pickett remembered hearing Caxton describe as "badly in need of redevelopment, like, someone should put a match to it," and wiped some crumbs off her front. "Siggy din't do it. He was home Friday night with me."

"Did anyone else see him?"

"No. He was home, though. He wasn't home Thursday 'cause we had a fight in the morning and I throwed him out. But he came back Friday."

"What time?"

"About nine."

"I think that gives him enough time."

"If he'd killed Marlow, I'd've knowed. But he din't act up like that. He acted ordinary."

She was convincing about her own conviction, at least. "Did he stay home all the time after that?"

"No way. He just come and went like always. And he was surprised at the news like I was. He din't kill Timmy Marlow."

He watched her trudge down the track to the road, wondering what he had taken on, wondering where he would start. He knew why he had said yes, but after she had disappeared from sight, it occurred to Pickett, in time to prevent him from congratulating himself at his charity in responding to her plea, that if she had been any other woman he would also have offered her a lift back to town. It hadn't occurred to him. Poor old broad.

CHAPTER 17

The first thing, he decided, was to tell Wilkie what he had agreed to do. That might be the end of it, as long as he was satisfied that there was no reasonable doubt. He needed to get his chain saw sharpened, too, a service that Nykoruk didn't offer, so he washed the dishes, microwaved a cup of old coffee, and drove into Sweetwater an hour later.

He found Wilkie in his office and told him what he had undertaken. Wilkie hardly reacted at all. "Private eye, eh, Mel? Like all you old farts who retire from the metro force."

"Just this once, Abraham, my boy. Pickett's Last Case. Then I'll close the agency." Pickett had been wary of Wilkie's reaction to what he might have seen as meddling, and although he was encouraged by the mildness of Wilkie's response, he stuck to the jocular tone he had decided on. It was probably good if Wilkie didn't take him seriously.

Wilkie shrugged, aimed a ball of paper at the wastebasket, and missed. "What do you want to know? What'll satisfy her?"

"Nothing. If I don't help, she'll try someone else. You

know the type. She'll go round and round, bugging everybody. So let me do what I can. What have you got against him?"

"You want me to tell you our case against Siggy? Okay. Everyone in Larch River knows it." Wilkie outlined the facts, and the reasonable assumptions that he had drawn from them.

Pickett said, "But it's still circumstantial, then."

"We're looking for the gun, which will have Siggy's fingerprints on it, and specimens of his hair, blood, and saliva, probably. That will wrap it up, I hope. We think Siggy might have been trying to blackmail Marlow, and any day now we expect him to break down and confess. But just in case we're wrong, we're also looking for anyone else who might have shot Marlow in the face. So far we've questioned and accounted for everyone in Larch River. But at the moment, yes, it's still circumstantial."

"Does Siggy seem like the kind to do it? I hardly knew the guy, even to see, but from what I've heard he wouldn't have taken Marlow on."

"I doubt if he did. I think it must have been nearly accidental, and if he'd reported it right away, we wouldn't have charged him with much. But he didn't report it, so we're entitled to think of manslaughter, at least, just because of the trouble he's caused us."

"If he did it."

"Who else?"

"Can I see him? Is he still here?"

"We have to ask him, fix a time."

"Today?"

Wilkie looked at his watch. "Let's try for three o'clock."

Relieved that Wilkie was making it so painless to respond to Mrs. Siggurdson's request, Pickett left his chain saw at the hardware store, filled up with gas at a cent a liter cheaper than Charlotte's boss sold it for, and returned to Wilkie just before three.

"You're not going to get to first base, Mel," Wilkie said. "He doesn't want to talk to you."

"Did you tell him I'm here because of his mother?"

"He says he didn't realize what she was up to. He's got nothing to tell you, he says. Leave him alone, is what he says."

"Can't I even take a look at the guy?"

"He's got the right to say no to that, too, I think, but we'll just spring you on him."

They walked through to the cell area. Siggy was lying on a bunk in the only occupied cell, a small, fat, semi-bald character dressed in a pair of greasy dark pants and a whitish T-shirt. His yellow boots were on the floor of the cell. Wilkie said, "This is Mr. Pickett, Siggy, the man your mom . . ."

"Fuck off," Siggurdson said.

"I was talking to your mother, Siggy," Pickett said.

Siggy stretched out and rolled on his side, away from them, his face resting on his hand. "Fuck off," he said.

"Sorry, Mel," Wilkie said, when they were back in the office. "Not a lot I can do for you. Or you for him, I guess." He was grinning.

"I'll just have to find the guy who did it."

Wilkie looked up at him without lifting his head. "What's that supposed to mean?"

"My client says her son didn't do it. So somebody

else must have." Pickett smiled to show he was barely serious.

Wilkie laughed. "You're going to give it a real try, aren't you? How do you plan to start?"

"Ask around. Find out who had it in for Marlow."

"Let me know when you find out, won't you? I've tried."

"You'll be the first to know."

It was wise to keep the tone jokey, but Pickett was now slightly intrigued. In the first place you would think that a man like Siggy, facing a manslaughter charge, would welcome all the help he could get. Siggy ought to be shaking the bars, protesting his innocence. It was possible that the reason why Siggy didn't want to talk to him was that he was in such deep misery, but then it was odd to find him calm, telling him to fuck off in such a vigorously dismissive voice. It was not much, but odd enough to make him want to stay around.

The problem was where to start. Siggurdson himself was the natural person to question about Marlow, about who his cronies were. After Siggy, the other obvious person to ask was Betty. And Caxton.

Pickett was glad of the excuse to call on Caxton, whose behavior was becoming a worry. He had apparently given up his one-man investigation altogether and gone into hibernation. He no longer patrolled the town, staying home unless he was called out by telephone. He seemed to be awake and moving inside the house at any time of the night that Pickett passed; during the day, he sat dozing in an armchair. All of this, Pickett assumed, was because he had lost Betty. The man needed someone to talk to, however tedious that might be.

When Pickett found him at home, in his office, Caxton was still consumed with the idea that Marlow had shaved his beard off for some good reason, and the only one that Caxton could come up with was that he was meeting someone and didn't want to be recognized.

"What does Betty think?" Pickett asked.

"Betty doesn't know anything. He told her he was going to Toronto, then he turned up dead here in Larch River. That's all she knows. She's still talking to me through the screen door." He twisted in his chair.

"What does Wilkie think?"

"Who knows what Sergeant Wilkie does or doesn't think about anything? I haven't asked, and he hasn't said. I'm right out of it. I do what he asks, and sometimes he asks me to come along and watch, and that's all. But that's all my problem. What can I do for you?"

Pickett said, "Mrs. Siggurdson came to see me. She thinks her boy is being shafted."

"Why you?"

"She can't find anyone else."

"Are you going to help her?"

"I don't have any status. She doesn't understand that, though, so I told her I would satisfy myself. I was impressed, Lyman. She calls Siggy a fuck-up herself, but she says there's no way he would go up against Marlow, and now I have a reasonable doubt, too. What do you think?"

The chief twisted back and forth. "I have to say she's got a point," he said. "I never thought that bag of lard would pull a trigger, ever."

Pickett said, "Somebody did. Who are Siggy's pals?"

"Wilkie would know by now. Siggy isn't about to be loyal to his associates if he would do better by ratting on them."

"So someone else. Not with Siggy. Who else was Marlow close to?"

"He didn't have anyone except Siggy. See, Timmy was kind of the lone wolf—no, that's not what I mean— he was a lone *operator*, never part of a gang. You'd see him in the beer parlor sometimes—there's two or three layabouts Siggy drinks with, but they'd be drunk and Timmy wouldn't, know what I mean? He did get drunk sometimes, but roaring drunk, not sitting around a table with a bunch of deadbeats. He thought he was Hud."

"And Siggy?"

"Siggy was his whatdoyoucallit—his servant, his asslicker, batman. He hung around Timmy, and Timmy let him. But most of the time Timmy was off chasing women, more and more in Sweetwater."

"And you don't know of any enemies he might have picked up."

"No, I don't, not lately. Most people gave him lots of room. He could be a mean son of a bitch. He beat up a guy real bad once in Sweetwater, more than he needed to."

"Will you see if his sister will talk to me?"

"Probably she won't." He dialed Betty's number, made Pickett's request, looked surprised, said, "He'll be right over," and then said to Pickett, "Apparently it's just me she won't talk to."

Before he left, Pickett said, "Lyman, don't sit brooding, thinking about her. Get out of here. Come up to my place for a beer, game of cards."

"Don't worry about me," Caxton said and sat down, turning to look out the window.

Betty Cullen was surrounded by cardboard cartons, which she was filling with wrapped glasses. The need to pack seemed to be helping her through the stress of Marlow's death. When Pickett had explained what he was there for, she said, "I don't see how you're going to get around Siggy. I wish it was someone I didn't know, but I guess it must have been him. No one saw anyone else, did they? Even Siggy hasn't claimed to. Anyway, leaving Timmy out there all weekend like that . . ."

"I know there's not much to be said for Siggy, as Siggy. But what his mother says rings true, that he doesn't have the guts."

"Did you speak to him?"

"He won't talk to me."

"Why?"

"I don't know." Another possible solution occurred to Pickett. "He thinks maybe I'm part of some police trick. Even though his mother came to me, he thinks I'm on their side, not his."

She looked at him sharply. "You mean he might know something he hasn't let out yet?"

"It's possible."

"What did you want to know from him?"

"Two things. First, to hear exactly what happened, step by step. Talking to me he might not be so uptight and he could remember something he's been leaving out, something that might work in his favor. The second thing was to see if he could help me put together your brother's world. The people he knew. That's why I've come to you."

"You mean who he hung around with lately, or in the past?"

"I wasn't thinking of the past. Lately, I guess."

"Timmy never confided in me. He wouldn't have, though, would he? I was like a mother in some ways, and you don't tell your mother about your women, do you?" She started to fidget.

Pickett got to his feet, but her question about the past stayed. "How long had Timmy been living in Larch River?"

"Seven years." She jumped up. "I could look it up. I've got the exact date in my daybook in the bakery. My journal. I use it as a diary. I'll look it up."

Pickett lifted his palm. "The day doesn't matter. Seven years is long enough to have acquired all the enemies he needed right here."

"The only one I know around here who hung out with Timmy was Siggy."

Pickett thanked her and left.

An hour later she called Pickett as he was opening a beer before supper. "I looked up that date you were wondering about. Timmy arrived in April 1988. I'll show you in the book."

"Thanks, that's good enough. Where did he come from, by the way?"

"Out west."

"From a town?"

"Winnipeg, I think. Why?"

"Did he ever hear from there? Or go and visit old friends?"

"He never had any money, not to pay for trips."

He put the phone down and looked at Willis, resisting the temptation to speak his surprise aloud. He was trying to avoid turning into a cute old fart who talked to his dog.

CHAPTER 18

By this point, Pickett had expected that he would have made up his mind already, almost certainly in agreement with Wilkie, but although he had not found a shred of real contradiction, collectively the people he had talked to so far had made him uneasy. Everything he knew and had heard about Siggurdson had made him assume he was a blubbering liar, desperate to convince someone that he did not kill Marlow; instead, an indifferent Siggy had told him to fuck off. Caxton seemed a little out to lunch on the whole issue, and Betty Marlow was a puzzling mixture of aggression and worry. Even Wilkie did not ring entirely true. His current placidity was not justified by the strength of his case, which a real lawyer ought to be able to shred easily. The only person of real conviction was Evie Siggurdson.

Until he noticed Linda McCourt, the girl seen with Marlow in the cottage, crossing the street, Pickett thought he was out of ideas, but seeing her he remembered her early statement and that gave him two more people to talk to. Linda McCourt was the first. He waited until she had gone back to work, and tackled her in her change booth.

At first she was hostile. She had been happy with the promise from Wilkie that the police would keep her involvement with Marlow quiet, especially from her father, but if Wilkie had kept his word then this man ought not to have known enough to find her. "The OPP tells me that I'm speaking to them in confidence," she said, nearly in tears. "Then they tell someone like you everything. I've got nothing to say to you. Get out of here."

"The OPP didn't tell me a thing. I got it from someone else who saw you with Marlow."

Her eyes became wet. "I suppose the whole frigging town knows. It's sure to get back to Dad. Oh, Jesus."

"Not from me. But, yeah, sure, you have to be ready for the chance that he might find out one of these days. But not from me or the OPP. And I'll ask the OPP to remind the guy who told me to keep his mouth shut."

"Dad'll kill me."

"They're not using your evidence. Only the OPP know your name. You'll probably be all right."

"Well, what do you want to know? I thought I'd said it all."

"I want you to tell me what kind of guy Marlow was. What you thought of him then. What you think of him now. Anything that might help me to know him a bit. Let's try a few possibilities. Was he cheap with his money? What did he think he was good at? What plans did he have? Who did he ever mention that you didn't know?"

He stayed there for an hour. They were interrupted eight or nine times by customers paying for gas, but in the second half hour he began to get close to his real interest. "Who were his friends?" he asked for the third time.

"He didn't have any except me. And Siggy."

"Did he call Siggy a friend?"

"He called Siggy a lard ass, but he let him hang around."

"Why did he stay in Larch River if he despised it so much?"

"His sister. He had a job."

"Baker's delivery boy?"

She snickered. "Right on. I called him something like that once when he was blowing about himself and he hit me across the room. I went back at him with a piece of stove wood. I wasn't going to let him think he could knock me around as if I was some little chippie he could do what he liked with. Then he said he was sorry. See, I'd injured his pride." She gave a wide, jeering smile.

A feisty little babe, Wilkie had called her.

"What else was he proud of?" Pickett asked.

"That's a good question. He was always talking about making a move, but he couldn't do anything. He didn't know anything. He couldn't even add properly."

"What did he do before he came here? Any idea?"

"Something to do with fishing, I think. I don't know."

"Where?"

"I don't know. He hardly ever said anything about it. Somewhere out west."

"Are you sorry he's dead?"

"You heard what happened, didn't you, how he left me up the creek? Course, I'm not sorry. Oh well, maybe a bit. We had some nice times together."

"Where?"

"In the cottage. We couldn't go out together, not around here. And you don't have a lot of choice in this place. I mean, I don't, except high school kids."

His other hope was Pat Dakin. He called at the bed-and-breakfast, the Linton House, in order to find her Toronto address, and she opened the door. "I'm sorry," she said in a tone that had nothing to do with regret. "We're not in the B-and-B business now."

For a moment he thought she recognized him from his brief stay more than two years before, but she had barely looked at him. "It's you I wanted, Mrs. Dakin. My name's Mel Pickett."

She stepped forward, looking confused. "Oh yes, the carpenter. You're building a cabin, I believe." She opened the door wide. "What can I do for you?" Now she stepped back. "Do you want to come in? I'm packing, so there won't be any coffee offered." She turned and swept away, leaving him to close the front door and follow her into the living room. "My husband and I are separating," she said over her shoulder. "He's not here. We have a schedule for packing that lets us avoid each other. There's a chair there if you want. Now, what can I do for you?" She looked around the room, her mind on her packing. "Hmm?" she asked, still looking around the room, when nothing was forthcoming.

"I wanted to ask you to tell me what you know about Timmy Marlow." Once again he anticipated having to get past the fear and hostility of someone who had hoped that she had heard the last of Marlow and Siggurdson. But Pat Dakin came from a class that attacked when it was upset.

There was a theatrical pause as she turned to face him. "You're a carpenter, you say. What else are you?"

Pickett explained his mission.

"I see. Right. I understand that I was identified by the killer as someone he once saw with Timmy. Because of this creature, the police felt they had a right to investigate my relationship with Timmy. I told them that on the night he was killed I was at a lodge, where he was supposed to join me. I was there from five o'clock until the next morning, identified a number of times by the owner. I came back here on Saturday and left for Toronto the same day. I suppose it was useful for the police to establish where he planned to spend the night. Now, though, I understand they have caught the man who killed him." She swung around to put her back to him. "And now, Mr. Retired Policeman, I am aware that I may find myself on a witness stand, and I'm not looking forward to that. I'm very much aware of what it will look like for a woman like me to be involved with a man like Timmy Marlow. People are going to snigger. So I cooperated with the police in the hope that they might be able to avoid using me at all at the trial. I felt that the sergeant was sympathetic. Now I see he is telling the world I was Marlow's mistress."

She turned back to face him. "Well, Mr. Carpenter, I am ignorant of police etiquette in these matters but I plan to find out if the statements of witnesses to the police are confidential or if they are public property, and if the former then I shall ask my lawyer what we might get for the damage I am now suffering in having to respond to the curiosity of outsiders like you, and everyone else the OPP have told about me." She ended on a high, metallic note, challenging him to respond.

Pickett said, "Mrs. Dakin, I'm not breaking any police confidences. I'm here because of something Eliza Pollock said. Marlow used to hang around the rehearsals, she said, until you dropped out. It's a natural conclusion that it was you he was interested in—he didn't make a pass at Eliza—and she said she thought she remembered you chatting to him a couple of times. So I thought you might be able to help me."

She came down to earth. "You mean you didn't know about my affair?"

"I mean that I heard about you from Eliza, who might have been gossiping from her own conclusions." Pickett was sweating slightly. He had not discussed the problem with Wilkie, but the sergeant would be very pissed off if he thought Pickett was giving the impression that he was in Wilkie's confidence. He would assume that Pickett knew enough to put aside anything Wilkie had told him about the people he had interviewed. Now that he was working for Mrs. Siggurdson he was entitled to know nothing.

Pickett believed he might have got away with this one. Thank God for Eliza.

Pat Dakin snorted. "And here I am giving you a full account, anyway. So now you know. What did you want?"

"Gossip. I want to know about Marlow's life. Here and outside Larch River. I'm looking for enemies, and I can't find them."

"All I know is that he managed the bakery."

If you believed he managed the bakery, then you are more gullible than Linda McCourt, Pickett thought. "Weren't you curious about him? He didn't grow up around here. Did he ever talk about where he came from, his plans or dreams? Any schemes he had?"

"He *was* restless. And ambitious. I'll tell you something rather silly. I think he wanted me because I wasn't part of his world. He admired my class, he said." She smoothed her skirt.

"That makes sense," Pickett said, and waited.

"But I can't think of a single thing he said which would suggest he had a world outside Larch River. He went into Toronto occasionally, but he had no friends there."

"He didn't want to move there?"

"I don't think he could move far away from the bakery."

Now they were getting nowhere. Pickett racked his brain for last questions. "Did he like his sister? Did they get on?"

"What a strange question. I think so. She doted on him."

"That's what everyone says."

"But when I was around them both, if I went into the bakery, for example, he seemed embarrassed, as if he was ashamed of her. Perhaps that was my fault." She thought about it. "Perhaps he was ashamed of me?"

"Did you give him any money."

"He wasn't a gigolo, if that's what you mean. I did *lend* him a little from time to time. Between paydays."

"Did he owe you when he died?"

"A few dollars. He was going to pay me back that weekend."

"Did you ever get together except in your cabin?"

"Not in the way you mean, no. One afternoon we went for a ride in my boat. Timmy tried to teach me how to fish. We only went out for an hour because I was afraid of being seen. He didn't care much, but he didn't have to. Now *there's* something I've just remembered. When we didn't catch anything I made fun of him, said he didn't know anything about fishing, and he got angry and said he was a professional. So I said why didn't he try for a job with the Black River Lodge, because he was always saying how he preferred to be outside. He said he'd taken a look at the lodge but it wasn't his kind of place. A two-bit operation, he said."

Pickett said, "One last question . . ."

"Were we ever caught? By my husband? No. He knows nothing about all this."

"Nothing?"

She colored slightly. "He knows I had a lover. I told him."

"When?"

"On Saturday morning, when I told him I was leaving him."

When Marlow was already dead.

Pickett rented a fishing boat from the marina, got some directions, and went for a ride upstream.

The name of the Black River Lodge was nailed to an upright at the end of the dock on the northern end of

Duck Lake. The lodge itself lay back from the lake, almost obscured by trees. Three boats were tied to the T-shaped dock: a launch with two sixty-horse motors, another, smaller boat with one fifty-horse motor, and an aluminum fishing boat with a twenty-five. Pickett stepped onto the dock and tied his boat to a ring. When he turned round, the owner was already walking down the dock, his hand extended in greeting. Pickett concluded that business was probably slow, the season having really finished by Labor Day.

"How are you today, chief?" the man said. "I'm Earl Ramsey." He looked at the boat Pickett had hired. "Did the marina send you up? You looking for a place to stay? I'm kinda booked up until the end of the week, but when did you want to come?"

Pickett jumped in quickly. "I came by to ask you about a man named Siggy Siggurdson."

Ramsey switched off the greeting. "I hear he's in jail for killing his buddy," he said. "What do you want from me? I used him a few times for fishermen. Sometimes I get a little bit of a rush on. Mostly me and the boy can handle all the business, but sometimes I'd ask Siggy to help out. He was generally free."

"Would you give him a character reference?"

"Who are you, mister?"

Pickett explained.

"I know about you. You're the retired cop who's building a cabin. How come you're mixed up with people like Siggy?"

"I'm not mixed up with him. I think he needs someone on his side, that's all."

"That'll be a change for him. Well, I can testify that Siggy did his work well, and never stole anything from here. How's that? Privately I can tell you that Siggy never stole anything because I never let him out of my sight when he came ashore, but that's beside the point, isn't it? I didn't trust him an inch, but he knew where the fish were, if there were any. Fact is, don't tell my American guests, but this whole area is pretty well fished out.

"I'm not surprised that Siggy's accused of killing Marlow, though I would have been less surprised if it had been the other way round, Siggy not being possessed of much in the way of balls for stuff like that. I don't think of him being connected with guns."

"Did you think of Marlow that way?"

"I'll tell you what I thought about him. Siggy brought him up one time when my boy was in Toronto, because I had a couple of Americans who wanted to come back in the spring and hunt bears. Usually I'd recommend them to talk to Lucas Fast, about ten kilometers from here, who's about the best bear-hunting guide in the county, but Lucas wasn't available so Siggy suggested Marlow. He seemed like a blowhard to me so I asked him if he'd ever taken people hunting before. He mentioned this camp then, a place called Bailey's on the Lake of the Woods. I happen to know Bailey, he runs a pretty classy fishing and hunting lodge, so I called him and he remembered Marlow. He'd worked for him a long time before, and Bailey remembered that he'd fired him because he beat up an Indian kid from the reservation. Bailey kicked him off the camp before a war started. And he said, as far as he remembered, Marlow had never guided hunters, just fishermen."

"So you never used him?"

"That's right."

CHAPTER 19

Now Pickett had a thread to pull, but before he looked any further, he had to check something else. He drove back to leave Willis at the cabin, and found Wilkie sitting in his car with Copps on the road outside. "Just stopped to see if you were home," the OPP man said. "I hear you've been talking to Mrs. Dakin."

When Pickett said nothing, he continued. "That's allowed, I guess. She says you told her I didn't send you. What else have you been doing today? One of my boys saw you on the river."

"Looking for driftwood, bodies, stuff like that."

"Uh-huh. Well, my other message should interest you. Siggy just pleaded guilty. Freely. A full and frank confession. We didn't put any pressure on him. Come and see him yourself. Not a mark on him."

"In the presence of his lawyer, I would imagine."

"Oh, yeah." Then, in a different tone, "I don't like his lawyer, either, Mel, but I just came up here to tell you that you're wasting your time. It's all over. We know what happened."

"Does Mrs. Siggurdson agree?"

Wilkie looked irritated. "What's she got to do with it?"

"She's my client."

"You'll be making an asshole of yourself, you know that?"

"Somebody will." Pickett returned to his car.

"Mel," Wilkie called sharply. "For your own sake, leave it alone."

"That'd be unethical, Abraham. What'll I do about my client?"

Wilkie and Copps watched him turn into the gate to his cabin. Wilkie said, "I've been fair, don't you think? I've tried. I hate to see him make a goddamn fool of himself, running around like this."

"Why? Let him fuck up. Be interesting to see if he comes up with anyone."

"Apart from Siggy, you mean?"

Copps nodded, grinning. "Won't be easy, will it?"

When the two OPP men had gone, Pickett drove into town to the hardware store, where Craig Thompson, Eliza's future Tony Lumpkin, served behind the counter. So far four fifty-dollar bills had surfaced, leading Pickett to wonder how common the denomination was in Larch River. He rarely handled one himself, and he remembered reading a story that the Bank of Canada itself was frustrated in its attempts to get the citizenry to use more fifties. The chief obstacle was that the new banking machines used the twenty as their basic unit, and something like 40 percent of the cash in circulation passed through the machines. As a result, Canada's was among the most inefficient currencies in the world, right down there with those of Turkey, Greece, and Ireland.

At the hardware store, Pickett held up three twenties. "I need a fifty-dollar bill," he said. "Sending it to someone. A christening gift. Looks nicer in one bill."

"If I have one." He lifted the cash register tray out and peered underneath. "Sorry, Mr. Pickett. I guess we haven't taken any in today."

"Not one? Business slow?"

"We've had a pretty good day." He grinned and dropped into the role of a country rube. "Folks around here don't trust the orange money. No, sir. We figure you could've made it yourself. My granddaddy got a counterfeit bill once and we ain't never forgot it. Varnished it, he did, and nailed it to the wall."

"You don't get many fifties, then?"

The boy resumed his normal persona. "One a week, maybe two. Try the service station. He gets the tourists, the Americans. City folks," he added with a brief last flash of the yokel.

But Pickett had learned what he wanted to know. He crossed the street to the bank, asking the teller if he could see the manager. She opened the gate and Pickett walked through to where Villiers was sitting behind his door, polishing his shoes with a duster.

"Busy?"

"Birdshit," Villiers said. "I've got a Rotary meeting in Sweetwater tonight straight from the office and a bird just shit on me. What can I do for you, Mel?"

"I was thinking about the money Siggy found on Marlow. Four fifties so far. That sound a little strange to you?"

Villiers spat on one of his toecaps and began a final shine. "You want me to speculate?"

"I thought you already might have."

"Let's see. There's a chance that Betty saved out all the fifties and gave them to Timmy. She doted on him, did you know that?"

"So you all say. And Timmy saved them up in his piggy bank?"

"That's less likely, I would think."

"How many would she take in?"

"Maybe one or two a week. From the wholesale customers mainly—the coffee shop, for instance. But if she gave them to Timmy, why wouldn't he spend them, like you suggest? He wasn't the saving kind. Didn't have piss-all in his account here. That's confidential, you understand."

"Maybe he stole them?"

"That does seem the most likely, doesn't it? She wouldn't turn him in to Caxton. Not for a fifty."

"Maybe she saved out all the fifties for a couple of weeks and he took them."

"Could be."

"Why? Why would she do that?"

"It's called skimming, Mel. Lot of small businesses do it. Big ones, too, but they call them directors' fees and executive bonuses. But the little guy does it to get even with the tax man, and as long as they keep to a pattern it's very hard to catch, especially in a one-person business, a ma-and-pa grocery store, or a little family bakery. Once you have employees, though, it gets harder because to make sure the employees aren't doing a little skimming of their own you have to put in safeguards, and those safeguards work against the owner, too. But you know all this. What it amounts to is that Betty could have set the fifties aside to have some spending money that the tax man doesn't know about, and little Timmy Marlow came across them, under the floorboards, and helped himself."

"That what happened, you think?" Pickett was just beginning to understand Villiers's style. An explanation like this was reasonable, but he might have others.

Villiers said, "All right, we've got there now. That door closed? No, since we've got there at last, I'll tell you what I've just found out. I've been sitting here wondering what I should do about it. Maybe you can help me.

"After we talked about that first fifty, I did a little thinking about it, then a little back checking. I looked at Betty Cullen's deposits this year—you say a word about this, I'll wind up outside Union Station with a tin cup—"

"I'm just curious. Like you. When did you do this checking?"

"About an hour ago. I was just about to call someone about it, you or the OPP."

(Thinking about it later, Pickett realized that Villiers had almost certainly been sitting for a couple of days with what he had found out, looking for someone to relieve him of it, when Pickett walked in and raised the subject.)

Villiers laced up a shoe and walked to the door to make sure no one was listening. "I'll tell you what I think. She hasn't held anything back. The same frequency of fifties as ever, just what you would expect. Business a little up on last year."

"So where did Marlow get the money?"

"Oh, from the bakery, all right. See, just before he was killed, the bakery's weekend deposit went missing. Should've been around two thousand, but it never came in. So I looked at the week before. Same thing. Altogether about four thousand missing."

"Marlow took it?"

"Who else? Betty didn't report a robbery, did she?"

"You tell Caxton this?"

"I just found it out, Mel. No, I didn't. Anyway, Betty knows. Let her tell Caxton. Or not. I reckon Timmy robbed his sister, though, and then got robbed himself." He looked down at his polished shoes, then inspected the rest of himself for lint. "Now I need a joke. I'm toastmaster tonight. Know any?"

"I heard a good one in England last year, or was it the year before? If I think of it, I'll call you. But before I go, I can't do anything with this information. Dumping it on me doesn't help you. Phone the bank's lawyers; find out what your duties and responsibilities are."

"I did. They said I should respond to all police inquiries."

"So. You haven't had any."

"But this may be important. Don't you think? You were a cop."

"Screw you, Ernie Villiers. All right. I'll see what's best. But if I do nothing, I don't want you shooting your mouth off to the OPP that you thought I had some official status around here, so you told me, thinking that was your duty done."

"I wouldn't land you in it, Mel."

"I think you already have."

It took Pickett an hour of brooding but eventually he found an approach and drove over to Caxton's office. He found the chief asleep on a couch. Caxton dragged himself upright without an apology and waited for Pickett to speak.

"I've been thinking," Pickett said. "From what you told me about seeing Marlow lift some cash from the till, and with Marlow maybe having to pay someone off, even Siggurdson, could there be any more money around? What I mean is, could Marlow have got hold of a lot more money from Betty's business without her knowing? Has she checked lately?"

"Wherever he got the money, I've been pretty sure from the start that Marlow was meeting someone that night. Remember?"

"Right, Lyman, so you have. Could this be the money that was supposed to change hands?"

"Better ask her yourself," Caxton said. "She won't talk to me." He rolled onto his back and closed his eyes.

To his astonishment, when he asked Betty Cullen, she responded immediately, first with violent anger, then with a confession. Pickett drove into Sweetwater immediately. In Wilkie's office, he said, "She really tore into me. Said that I knew goddamn well, or you did, that they'd found the money, and they—*you*, that is—were trying to trick her. Said the money you'd found was what she gave to Timmy to buy a new car with. He could get it much cheaper for cash, she said, and if she didn't report the income she'd save some on taxes. So for once she'd done something illegal and right away she'd got caught." He paused. "I was trying to get a message through to her, that if Marlow had stolen a lot from her, she shouldn't try and cover it up. It might help the police to know. I'm glad that's not true, but what is true is something you should know. There is a lot of money involved."

"How much?"

"Four thousand, she says."

"It hasn't turned up. But we'll find it somewhere in Siggy's yard."

"You still think Siggy did it?"

It took some time for Wilkie's answer to reach his lips. "Brendan has an idea. Let's get him in here." He avoided Pickett's eye while they waited. When Copps appeared, Wilkie explained quickly the point the conversation had reached.

Copps took a chair and said, "I think it's blackmail."

Pickett said, "Everybody tells me Marlow wouldn't have cared a pinch of coonshit. The women might've, but seriously, you think he got four thousand off his sister to pay off Siggy?"

"To pay off somebody, yes, and I'll tell you why." Copps gave himself the air of a man with some news to impart. "Maybe not Siggy, but I'll tell you why it makes sense that Betty Cullen gave Marlow four thousand to shut someone up."

Copps's desire to milk his story had given Pickett a glimpse of where he was going. "You making this up?" he asked, in anticipation of what Copps was going to say.

"I've wondered from the beginning. Everyone around here tells us she doted on him. After about the tenth *dote* I started to wonder what the word meant."

"I wouldn't let Lyman Caxton in on what you're thinking. He's on the edge now. He'd take an ax to you."

"It makes sense, though, doesn't it? Suppose Siggy or someone caught Marlow and his sister in the sack, just by chance. Tell you the truth, I wondered at one point if maybe Caxton had."

"You can stop wondering about that. In fact, you can forget the whole goddamn script."

"It may not be so bad. It may not even be illegal."

"What the hell are you talking about?"

"We only have her word that he *was* her brother, don't we?"

"Christ Almighty." He turned to face Wilkie. "You asked Siggy about this?"

Wilkie, uncomfortable, said, "I don't want to—what do they call it?—lead the witness. Put words in his mouth. Anyway, if Siggy doesn't volunteer it, I couldn't prove it. It's just something that occurred to Brendan when we were trying to make sense of everything that's going down. Even if he *was* her brother, there's a lot of stuff goes on in these small towns, Mel."

"If I were you, old son, I'd prove it before I talked about it."

"I'm just telling you what was in my mind," Copps said.

"That right? Thing like this would feel at home there, I guess."

Copps shrugged, looked inquiringly at Wilkie, and left.

"You really believe this?" Pickett asked.

Wilkie looked at his hands. "As soon as someone suggests something, it becomes a possibility, Mel."

CHAPTER 20

The Larch River *Gazette* was written and printed in Sweetwater. It was a weekly community paper, thirty pages thick, most of it given over to advertising. The news was all of local events, which took up the front pages and three or four columns dotted through the pages of advertising. The news gatherer was the wife of the town doctor, Helen Kuntz, who wanted to be a writer and used the *Gazette* for practice. She gathered up the news of what was officially happening and received all the requests for publicity for the town's social events. Twice a week she drove to Sweetwater, where she and the publisher together wrote the paper. The publisher owned six such newspapers in that part of Ontario, and one press served them all.

Pickett had invented a good reason for reading the old files of the paper, a reason that grew out of his new interest in the survival of the twenty-dollar bill. What he pretended to want was some concrete information about the differences in prices between 1953 and today. He explained his mission to Vernon Calais, the publisher, who became intrigued. "How about doing a little story for me on it?" he asked. Pickett told him not to be silly, but agreed to pass on the information he found. "That'll do," Calais said, and led him to the archives. "Would be nice if they were on microfiche. But you'll just have to manhandle the originals."

It wasn't difficult. In 1953 the Larch River *Gazette* had begun as a four-page flyer consisting of a page of news and three pages of advertising. It took only minutes to flip through a year. Pickett stayed there all afternoon. First he diligently drew up a comparison list of groceries to give to Calais for his story, then he jumped ahead twenty years. If Siggurdson was to be believed, someone had shot Marlow at point-blank range and left without robbing him, either because he was disturbed, or because he was there to kill Marlow, not to rob him. Assuming the second, then Marlow had enemies that Wilkie had not heard about.

First he established when Marlow had really arrived in town. This turned out to be easy, because from about twelve years before, some attempt had been made to make the *Gazette* look more like a newspaper by adding, on the back pages, a quarter page of "sports"— baseball in summer and hockey in winter—and on page two a small gossip column listing the social activities of the residents, including their comings and goings. Seven years ago the column had reported that the well-known bakery owner, Betty Cullen, had a guest staying with her, her young brother, Timmy, newly arrived to help out in the thriving business. After that, Pickett skimmed all the way to the current issue, just in case there was anything about Marlow, or his sister, or Siggurdson, but there was nothing.

He handed over the 1953 price list to Calais, who had already written the story. He showed Pickett the headline: SOME THINGS COST MORE FORTY YEARS AGO.

"Find any that did?" he asked, running his eye down the column.

"Television sets. Safety razors. Ballpoint pens."

"Perfect," Calais said.

Now Pickett made arangements for a little outing. Mrs. Siggurdson had given him the excuse he had been seeking for some time, a reason for taking one last ride on the Transcontinental train before they junked it. Everyone who knew him understood.

First he made a call to an old buddy in the Bail and Parole unit and asked him to ask his computer if there was any record of Timmy Marlow. The reply came back almost immediately. "He's dead. Homicide victim in a place called Larch River. Hey, isn't that where your cabin is? What are you up to, Mel?"

"I'm thinking of opening a detective agency. I'm practicing. I know he's dead, I'm trying to find out if he had a record."

"What the hell you talking about, practicing?"

"Put it this way. I'm trying to show the OPP how to do their job."

"You'll find your nose out of joint if you're not careful."

"They know what I'm doing. They think I'm on a wild goose chase. Look, Joe, it's a complicated and interesting little story, and when I come back I'll drop around and fill you in, but right now would you look up

'T. Marlow' on the machine and tell me what you find? And keep your voice down."

A minute passed. "Nothing," Joe said. "That end it?"

"Yeah. No. Keep it to yourself till I get back."

"Keep what? Back from where?"

"Christ, Joe, I'm trying to get a little confidential information, that's all. If anyone asks, tell them. But they won't. All I'm asking is that you don't phone the Sweetwater OPP and say, 'You know what? I got a call from Mel Pickett today about that homicide, Timmy Marlow.' "

"Okay, okay. I can keep a secret. Tell me when it's unclassified." He hung up.

The next day, Pickett left Willis with his librarian neighbor in Toronto and took the train to Winnipeg.

It was not easy to get a ticket. This was mid-September, the peak season, and he was told that the train was booked solid until November. If you wanted to travel in September, they said, you should book in April. But what about no-shows? he asked. Yes, that happened, they agreed. So he stayed in his own house in Toronto for the night and the next morning packed a bag and went down to Union Station to make his request in person. Now the lady at the information desk took pity on the poor old man who was afraid of flying and told him to come back in half an hour.

Pickett found a seat on a bench five feet away and sat down and looked sadly at the lady at the information desk until she called him over and told him she had found him a coach seat from Parry Sound to Winnipeg.

Parry Sound, he calculated, was three hours by car from Toronto, and even allowing another hour to get back to his house and get on the road, he had plenty of time to intercept the train. He explained his plan to the woman, who looked at him admiringly. "Lotsa time," she agreed. "You've got more than six hours." She grinned. "Wanna gamble? Wait another half hour, see if I can get you a seat to Parry Sound?"

Pickett guessed that with her on his side it was a good bet, so he bought a newspaper and went back to the bench, and half an hour later she asked him to hang on for five more minutes, and then she had it.

"Can I get a berth?"

"Now you're being greedy," she said, sadly. "Don't make me feel bad."

"No sweat. I'll take it."

He could sit up in the coach all night if necessary—you had to when you flew to Europe—but the way his luck was running, it might not be necessary.

And so it proved. He told the conductor about his need, and an hour and a half after the train left Toronto, right after Barrie, Pickett had a lower berth. That taken care of, he found a seat in the club car and ordered the first of two beers he would allow himself before Sudbury Junction, happy again at the prospect of looking at northern Ontario for two days through the windows of an air-conditioned train.

Pickett was a sentimentalist who hated the government for, among other things, what seemed to him the systematic destruction of Canada's great railway system. The Transcontinental had been cut back from a daily to something that ran three times a week, and Pickett, like a lot of other people, feared that the cutback was simply a prelude to a complete closing down of the system. Every instinct and desire cried out against it. From any point of view, the building of the railway from coast to coast had been a wonderful achievement, helping to create Canada by uniting it, and the great trains had become symbolic of the country. On his war service in England, Pickett had discovered that the words *Canadian Pacific* had a resonance for the English, a romantic power every bit as strong as phrases like *Yankee Clipper, Orient Express*, and *Flying Scotsman*.

He had himself traveled on the train several times on vacation before being lured to Europe like everyone else by cheap air fares. The first time, though, was when as an enlisted man in the RCAF he had been shipped from Toronto to Halifax, across Quebec and the Maritimes. It was the first time he had gained a real feel for the country he was born in. After the war he had traveled with his wife to Vancouver, across northern Ontario (his favorite bit because in places you could still see the world that the first settlers saw, uninhabitable and beautiful), then over the prairies (nice at sunset) to the Rockies (a disappointment), and on through the interior of British Columbia to the Pacific. He had never done the whole seven-day, coast-to-coast journey in one trip and now he probably never would, but when he thought of Canada he thought of the railway, a line stretching from the Atlantic to the Pacific with ten different landscapes strung along it.

He wondered what sort of image the next, non-train-riding generation would have, no doubt already had. A field of ice seen from thirty thousand meters up? Or a gray-green carpet pocked with holes full of water from the same height? He had often thought that no one should be granted citizenship until they had traveled across the country by train, at the taxpayers' expense. Such a scheme, he thought, would ignite a valuable chauvinism and help to make the railway economically viable. But what about the native-born Canadians who had never taken the train? Soon there would be too many of them, too. Maybe you could demand it of the MP's, at least? Cabinet ministers, maybe? Any day now, he mused, we would find ourselves in the hands of a prime minister who had never ridden the train, and that would be the end of it.

Another instinct than the romantic told Pickett that dismantling railways of any kind was stupid and short-sighted, and exactly like the way the big automobile interests in the United States. had destroyed the trolley-car systems in the thirties. A new generation of Canadians would one day curse his own for letting the railroads rust. But he never tried to argue the case. He was just glad of an excuse to take a train ride.

CHAPTER 21

They reached Winnipeg late the next afternoon, and Pickett checked in at the Marlborough Hotel. He had never visited Winnipeg before, and he could think of nothing he wanted to see. Winnipeg, he understood from people who had been born there, was a good town to grow up in, but there was not much for the tourist or visitor. The following morning he rented a car and drove the hundred miles back to Kenora.

The office of Bailey's camp was on a gravel back road, dead-ending in a cleared space where half a dozen cars with American license plates were parked in a square. Pickett strolled over to read the names of the states and a voice spoke behind him. "Need any help?"

He turned and saw a tall, weathered man in his forties, dressed as if for hunting, standing outside the door of Bailey's office. He looked as if he had just showered and shaved, and at the same time had the air of someone who might have been playing poker all night but didn't show it. Pickett walked over and waited for him to step aside to let him into the office, but the man stood in possession of the door, not blocking it but showing by his stance that he would be happy to answer Pickett's questions on the step. What did he want?

"Hi, there," he said.

"I'm looking for the owner or manager."

"I thought you might be looking for a car. You seemed to be sizing them up."

"I brought one of my own." Pickett nodded down the street. "You stand and watch all day? You must have a lot of car thieves in this town."

"Somebody stole one last week, and now the police are bringing it back and I have to find someone to drive it down to Minneapolis. I saw you through the window, so I thought I'd come out and say hello. I'm the owner. Harry Bailey. What can I do for you?"

Pickett said, "I'm trying to find someone who worked for you seven years ago. Or rather, I'm trying to find out something about him. I know where he is."

"Who would that be?"

"Timmy Marlow. He'd be about twenty-two then."

Bailey frowned, then, as the name registered, looked uninterested. "I remember Marlow. I fired him. What else do you want to know? How about identifying yourself, by the way. Which outfit you work for?"

Pickett explained himself and his mission. "Point is, I'm retired from the Toronto police. A woman in this little town where I have a summer cabin has come to me for help. Her son's in jail on suspicion of homicide. These people, both of them, are deadbeats, real unattractive family, but the case against him isn't black-and-white, and she's got no one else."

Bailey walked down the little flight of steps. He said,

"I don't want to go inside because the office staff will listen to us instead of working and we're real busy. Come on down to the hotel, and we'll have a cup of coffee."

In the coffee shop of the Kenricia Hotel, Bailey said, "I assume this guy you've got in jail did kill Marlow."

"Oh, I think so. That's what it looks like."

"So what are you searching back seven years for?"

"Because I can't find any other killers around town and because—although I think the killer probably is in the Sweetwater lock-up—I found a little discrepancy about some dates. Marlow's dead, but I think someone's trying to cover up his past. Maybe it caught up with him. And maybe this is all bullshit and all I'm doing is creating an excuse to ride the train, which I haven't done for years. And visit the Lake of the Woods. It's nice here."

"God's country," Bailey said automatically. "Come fishing. I'll give you a deal." He quoted a price for three days' fishing.

"Jesus. Do I get to keep the boat?"

Bailey laughed. "No, and you have to buy your minnows."

"People pay that, do they?"

"I'm booked up."

"Americans?"

"We had a Canadian here in the spring, I think. Or maybe that was last year. So, what can I do for you?"

"Tell me when Marlow worked for you and what you remember about him."

"I'll have to look up the dates. But I remember the guy very well. He worked for me for part of the summer. I'll look it up. Then I got rid of him."

"Why?"

"He beat up one of the Indian boys. A kid, maybe sixteen, who worked around the camp. Marlow was maybe five or six years older, and forty pounds heavier, and tough. He was in good shape."

"Why did he hit the kid?"

"It was something about a tip. Marlow was learning to be a guide, and he'd just finished a three-day trip with a couple of guys who looked good for a big tip. Before they left they told him they'd given the tip to an Indian boy to give to him. But when they'd gone, the kid said they didn't leave him any money. Then someone told Marlow he'd seen one of the guests give this Indian kid money on the dock, when they were waiting for the plane. So the next day Marlow took the kid to a quiet spot in the woods and beat the shit out of him. We had to get the doctor to him. Then one of the other guides said that he'd seen the incident, that the guest had given the kid a two-dollar bill for carrying his bags to the plane, and that anyway it wasn't Marlow's guest at all; it was some other guy. So I got rid of Marlow. Even if he hadn't shown himself to be such a vicious son of a bitch, I didn't want a war on my hands, not even a little one. Everybody liked that kid; I used him for carrying bags, and as a kind of bellboy because he was popular, he looked cheerful. It wasn't just the guests; all the other workers liked him. Marlow could have wound up with a tomahawk in his back. I'm just kidding. No, I'm not. So I put Marlow on the next plane to town."

"When was that?"

"We'll have to look it up in the office."

"What happened to him?"

"He went to Winnipeg, then disappeared. He was never much in my mind after that, but I got a call last year from a guy who runs a camp up your way, asking for a reference for Marlow. I didn't give him one, but I asked around to see if anyone had ever seen him again, and someone said he'd just disappeared. I guess he went in search of work."

"He had a sister who owned the bakery in Larch River."

"Where?"

"Larch River. Where I'm from. Where Marlow went. Where he got killed last week."

Bailey thought for a moment. "I doubt if it comes back to here. But if you see any strange Indians in, where? Lark River . . . ?"

"Larch River."

"Right. Ask them where they come from. Come on back to the office now and we'll look him up."

In Bailey's office they were able to consult his records without interrupting the staff, and Pickett wrote down the details on a slip of paper. "Left here July sixteenth," he repeated as he wrote it down. "There's a forwarding address."

"Can you tell me anything else about him?"

Bailey walked across the room to a two-way radio that had begun talking, reminding him that if he didn't get back to the camp soon there would be no ice left by morning. As he talked back he waved at Pickett to indicate that was all the time he had for the policeman.

Then, as Pickett was leaving, Bailey said, "Come for a ride. I've got to take a couple of fan belts up to the camp."

To Pickett's surprise, "a ride" meant a flight. They drove down to the town dock and climbed into a tiny bush plane with Bailey's legend on the side. They took off without fuss and soared above the Lake of the Woods, circling north.

The land below became mostly lakes and rivers, separated by patches of bush with, here and there, gray bulges of glacial rock. "Like it?" Bailey shouted above the noise of the engine.

"It's fantastic. What's that down there?" He pointed to a huge log building surrounded by a dozen cabins.

"Minaki Lodge. Pretty, isn't it? The railway built it in the thirties to encourage passengers. Got its own golf course, see? Changed hands a lot since then. I think the government had to take it over finally. Not economically viable." He leaned back and put his hands behind his head. "Wanna try flying it?"

"I just do that in video games. We're going *down*, for Christ's sake."

Bailey laughed and straightened the plane up. "So what else do you want to know?"

Pickett waited a minute to be sure Bailey didn't try to loop the loop. "First, you sure he was working for you in May?"

"Oh yes. He was on the payroll from the middle of the month, ready for the pickerel season, which opens toward the end of May."

"Was he a professional guide?"

"That was his first season, I think. But guiding from Circle Lake isn't very tricky. It isn't really guiding, not in the real sense. Just driving fisherman around to where the fish are. Course, it *looks* like guiding to people from Detroit, say. Marlow could have picked up enough in a week to get by. In a month he would have looked like a professional, unless he got into an emergency."

"Would there be people around who would remember him?"

"Maybe Henry Goose or Joe Littledeer. I don't think I have any white guides from seven years ago. They come and go. Hang on." He put the plane into a shallow descending curve and flew low over a small lake. "I crashed here once," he said. "Ran out of gas."

Pickett looked down at the tiny patch of water. "Is there enough room?"

"Just. I had to unload everything and take a run at it."

"Christ. How's your gas gauge now?"

They landed at Circle Lake and Bailey disappeared with the fan belts. Half an hour later they were in the sky again, on their way back to Kenora.

"I asked a couple of the guys if anyone had heard of your boy," Bailey said. "No one had except Damon Whitetail. He hasn't seen him since he left camp, but he remembered him. A mean son of a bitch, he said, but we knew that."

At the dock in Kenora, there was a small party waiting for them. Two fishermen and a camp worker on their way to the camp. Bailey became the professional host as soon as his feet touched the dock, leaving Pickett to look after himself.

He drove back to Winnipeg, counting the pluses: the view from the train and the view from the air. What more could you want? Learning about Marlow's background had become almost secondary to the good time he was having.

CHAPTER 22

The address on the slip turned out to be a rooming house in the north end of the city, on a street of tired and damaged houses. There was an old washing machine in the front yard of the house Pickett was looking for, and a pile of broken furniture stacked on one end of the porch. Pickett did not see much hope of furthering his research here, but the woman who answered the door seemed much less rundown than her house. She was thick-bodied, about sixty, he thought, but with the long yellow hair of her youth. She agreed immediately that she remembered Marlow.

"Sure," she said. "I remember everyone. Good-looking boy." She flexed her arms and rippled her shoulders in imitation of Marlow's muscularity. "What do you want to know? Come into the kitchen." She held the door open and led him to a chair at the kitchen table. She picked a shred from between two teeth and spat into the sink. "*Fleisch*," she said. "*Cochon*. Meat. I speak five languages." Then, "He in trouble? He only stayed a couple of weeks. I'll show you." She ran into another room and returned with a handful of cheap receipt books. "I keep everything," she said. "Had a goddamn tax audit once." She flipped back and forth, then said, "Here. He came July 17." She flipped ahead. "See, he stayed one more week, then he was gone."

"Was he broke?"

"Sure. Why else would he leave?"

"Would you carry him until he got a job?"

"Him and everybody else? Pay in advance or leave. Nothing else works in this end of town. I don't remember him not paying, though. Maybe he just left."

"Did he have any friends in the house? Or any who called in?"

"I don't remember any, but I don't allow friends past the front step. They have to wait outside. I'm pretty sure he was by himself. He might have had to share a room with someone here, but who knows who that would be after all this time? Is he in trouble?"

"He's dead."

"That could be a problem for him. What's it all about?"

"I'm trying to find out who killed him."

"You a cop? I thought so. We get a lot round here." Suddenly she stood up. "Well, lotsa luck. If you don't need a room, I got work to do."

Pickett wondered if he had done something wrong; once she had heard his business, she lost interest. In this part of north Winnipeg, people appeared and disappeared all the time.

Now Pickett moved on to the library of the Winnipeg *Free Press*. He was not sure what he was hoping to find, but he would know it when he saw it: some reason, a significant unsolved crime, perhaps, that caused Marlow to leave town in a hurry and bury himself in Larch River. He suspected that the item he was hoping to find would occur at the end of July, but he started on July 16 and read forward for a month. After two complete readings he had found nothing: then, the third time through, he found the story of the armed robbery of a convenience store. A man had been caught, his occupation given as a fishing guide. Pickett read the item carefully. Two men wearing face masks had robbed a ma-and-pa store and killed the owner, a Chinese named David Poon. The killer had panicked and dropped the cash box as he fled, but the other man had tripped and been grabbed by a passerby, who held him until the police came. Paul Devereaux was charged with attempted robbery and manslaughter.

With the help of the newspaper's librarian and a computer, Pickett followed the fortunes of Devereaux all the way to the trial, when he received ten years in Stony Mountain. After the first three newspaper stories, there had been no mention of the other man. He spent a further hour reading, but he could find no other crime that fitted so well what he was looking for, and he crossed his fingers and went back to his room to make a phone call.

So far Pickett had gone around the Winnipeg police, hoping to work quietly, but now he needed to know if Devereaux was still in jail, and he should start looking for someone else. He was trying to avoid having Devereaux's name go back to Wilkie until he was ready, because

Wilkie would know right away what Pickett was up to and raise the country looking for Devereaux. That was his job.

He would try the jail first.

He called Stony Mountain and identified himself as Sergeant Mumble of the Bail and Parole unit in Toronto. He had received a query, he said, about a man named Devereaux that should have come to them. That is, the computer showed that Devereaux was still in Stony Mountain Penitentiary. Or was he on parole? Could they confirm that?

No problem, the guard said, and then, three minutes later, said that neither was strictly true; Paul Devereaux had been granted parole a couple of months ago, but he had not reported as he should last week and therefore, being in breach of parole, he would go back inside when they found him. A message to keep an eye out for him had gone across the country; that was the message that had probably landed on Pickett's desk, the guard said.

Pickett put down the phone, praying that the guard would be sufficiently uninterested not to tell his superiors about the call, because they would probably find it very much stranger than he did. Pickett went down to the bar, drank a beer and ate some pretzels, then ate some liver and bacon in the restaurant and walked back to his room to make a start on the last volume in the Poldark series, trying not to think, unable to avoid knowing that what he had just heard was not the end, but the beginning.

Early the next morning, Pickett called Bailey's office again. Bailey was not in from the lodge yet; he stayed at the lodge until all the guests were safely out on the lake, fishing, usually about nine o'clock, then flew in to the office. Pickett asked the clerk to leave a message for Bailey to phone him, and went back to reading Poldark. Bailey called at nine-thirty. "What's up?" he wanted to know. "Not too long, though; I've got people here waiting to fish."

"Just a quick one. Did you ever hire a guy named Paul Devereaux?"

"I did indeed. A long time ago. Want to know where he is now? Try Stony Mountain. He's doing a stretch for manslaughter."

"Bad bugger?"

"Funny you should ask. No. I remember thinking at the time that it must be some kind of accident. Breaking and entering, a little thieving, sure. All of that. But shooting someone? I wouldn't have thought that was in Devereaux's repertoire."

"Why wasn't he working for you at the time? It was mid-summer."

"I'm not sure. No bad reason if he wasn't. I think he was trying to make a regular life for himself in the city. He wanted to settle down, get a twelve-month-a-year job. Maybe he wanted to get married. I think he drove a truck for a plumbing company that went bankrupt and he was out of a job, and his girlfriend left him. He had a drinking problem, I think. He asked me if he could come back, but I had a full team and, obviously you don't know about fishing, Mr. Pickett, but July and August are my slack times. I need extra people in May and September. So I couldn't use him, and next thing I know he's in jail. Look, I have to go. You'll find Devereaux in Stony Mountain."

"He's out now. On parole. One last question: were he and Marlow pals?"

"Jesus Christ. Now I know why you're looking for Devereaux. I remember at the time wondering who the other guy was. Hang on, I've got to stroke a couple of guests. Give me a few minutes."

Pickett heard him put the phone on his desk, and the sound of his voice being cheery to someone else. When he returned, he said, "They were pals, yes. I don't know why I didn't think of this before. See, Devereaux was kinda slow. Not retarded, but he liked to take things one at a time, you know? But he was a helluva good guide, and when Marlow came up I got Devereaux to look after him, show him the ropes. Devereaux took a job like that very seriously, and he worked at looking after Marlow. Then, the way I remember it, Devereaux went to town and it was just after that that I fired Marlow. If Devereaux's out he would go looking for his old pal, I would think. He'd have a score to settle."

"I was wondering how he got out there. He's not supposed to leave town, so he wouldn't have wanted to use the trains, even if he could have gotten a ticket, and he wouldn't have wanted to go through the airport. Winnipeg's a pretty small town . . ."

"Don't let them hear you say that."

"He wouldn't want to risk being seen by one of the cops he's come up against."

"So?"

"He couldn't rent a car, unless he used false ID. And

a man of his age would have trouble hitchhiking these days, even if he could avoid being picked up by the highway patrol."

"Speed it up, chief, will ya? This is interesting but I've got a line up here. So he probably stole a car."

"That's what I thought."

"It'll turn up. Best of luck. *Hey*! You mean Devereaux's the guy who stole the car off our parking lot? Where's Huntsville? Near Lark River?"

"Larch River."

"That's where they found it. Huntsville."

"Huntsville could be on the way to Larch River."

"Son of a bitch. Why didn't someone ask me? No, they did. I said all along it was probably someone who knew that those cars would not be missed for a few days. He'd have a head start." Bailey laughed. "This'll be a story for the local cops."

"Do me a favor. Keep it to yourself for a couple of days. Three. When they start looking for Devereaux and come to you for a description, then you can tell them you suspected all along."

"Why?"

"Let's just say I'd like to work with it by myself for a couple of days."

There was a silence, then a long laugh. "You're doing this on your own, right? You don't have any authority. But you know something the boys in the office don't, and it could bring you some moola, or prestige, or maybe you just want to poke someone up the ass." He laughed. "Sure. I'll make you a deal. You give me a call when it's over, tell me exactly what's happened, you hear? I could tell this story round the fire for the next ten years. My guests'll love it. Now I have got to go. There are two millionaires sitting on a little wooden bench outside, and at the moment they think that's backwoods and cute, but they won't for much longer. So you call me, you hear?"

"Wait a minute. One last thing," Pickett pleaded.

"I hope those guys outside don't have piles. What?"

"Did Devereaux leave an address with you?"

"Jesus, hold on." He repeated the question to someone in the office, then came back on the line. "Here. His sister, I think." He reeled off an address in Fort Garry, a Winnipeg suburb, and a telephone number. "That's it," he concluded. "Now can I go?" He hung up.

Pickett dialed the number of Devereaux's sister. "I'm a friend of Paul Devereaux," he said.

A male voice said, "Then if you see him, tell him I'll set the dogs on him if he comes around here again," and put the phone down.

Pickett waited half an hour and tried again, hanging up when the same man answered. He waited an hour the next time, and this time a woman answered. "This is Paul's case officer," Pickett said. "I think we've got a line on something he'd be interested in. Do you know where I can find him? He doesn't seem to be in the halfway house anymore."

"I don't know. He came around here when he got out of prison and I gave him a few dollars, but then my husband said I wasn't to speak to him or see him again. Or anybody else connected to him. I gotta go." She hung up.

*　　　*　　　*

The train left Winnipeg at one forty-five, traveling through northwest Ontario under a clear sky. All afternoon Pickett was content to watch the brilliant red and gold foliage, and its reflection in the blue of the lakes and the rivers.

He avoided the other passengers to give himself space and time to think about how he was going to tell Wilkie that he was probably holding the wrong man for the homicide, though not for robbing the body. Pickett had muddled his way to a much likelier suspect and he didn't think Wilkie would be pleased. But the chain of evidence in favor of the conclusion that Devereaux was their man was very strong. He wished he had been free to talk to someone who remembered the circumstances of Devereaux's arrest and conviction, but now that Devereaux was again wanted by the police, he had to guess. Two men had robbed the store and only one was caught, so it was no great feat to guess that Devereaux had refused to tell them Marlow's name, and had therefore endured a heavier sentence for his loyalty.

But the trial evidence showed that it was the other man who had had the gun; it was his fingerprints on the cash box, too, the prints the police had had for seven years, looking for the owner. And the second man had disappeared—with the gun. Marlow had left his rooming house two days later, presumably after a period of funk, realizing then that he had not been identified by Devereaux for his part in the robbery. He had one place to go, to his sister in Larch River. He had no money to get there. Did he hitchhike? Probably not. Perhaps a phone call to Larch River had got him his fare. And when he arrived, did he tell Betty what he had done? Or later, perhaps? Because at some point she had tried to construct an alibi for him by altering the date of his arrival in her daybook. But that wouldn't have worked until recently, when the day of his arrival had faded from the memories of the locals. In fact she might have been shielding him for the whole seven years, which would account for her refusal to marry Caxton. She could never be certain that one day he would not have to assist in the arrest of her brother for homicide. (On the other hand, she had just agreed to marry Caxton, and had given Marlow his marching orders.)

When he was tired of thinking, Pickett moved to the club car in search of conversation. Most of the passengers were retired Americans with whom he had something in common, and he looked forward to a chat about the old days, but almost immediately he was joined by an English journalist who was writing a story about the train for his newspaper. He was already three-parts drunk, and after a couple more drinks he became deeply sentimental about "this incredible vastness, I mean this stunning wilderness untouched except by seaplane."

Pickett corrected his terminology, although he wasn't sure, now, if the right term was bush plane or float plane. Inevitably they moved on to talk of the *voyageurs*, those Quebec traders, singing and paddling their way for two thousand miles across the land, long before the advent of bush pilots, and Pickett tried to remember one of their songs. By the time dinner was announced, the journalist was in tears at the beauty and wonder of it all.

As the train reached Sioux Lookout, around eight in the evening, he realized that Marlow's death should have been a relief to his sister, however much she doted on him. Her duty done, surely she could marry Caxton now. Did Lyman Caxton know? Probably not. He didn't have the guile or the will to handle a major deception. Caxton was a good man: not so much naturally virtuous as law-abiding; a policeman who would follow the rules with a punctiliousness that would be a pain in the ass to a colleague who saw a chance for a shortcut. He liked being the embodiment of law and order, and he might even have given up Betty rather than get involved with her problem with Marlow. If he had seen it coming.

Pickett climbed into his bunk and helped himself to a large scotch from his flask, but when he woke up, during a half-hour stop in Hornepayne, his mind was still on Caxton. What about now? After his first shock, any sorrow Caxton felt would have been tempered with a big helping of relief. But Betty would see the new danger; her brother was dead but his killer wasn't, and when they caught him the whole story would come out, and her shame would be complete, or whatever other nonsense she lived by. Because it *was* nonsense, Pickett thought. Times had changed; the world had other things on its collective mind than Timmy Marlow, and the scandal would soon fade. But for her, even with Timmy dead, the issue of respectability was still so strong that she must be hoping that Devereaux would escape.

CHAPTER 23

And then, crossing the French River on the way to Parry Sound in the middle of the afternoon, looking down at the water route the *voyageurs* had taken three centuries before, Pickett saw that Betty Cullen must have known from the time Devereaux first appeared who he was, had known and helped her brother to respond. The money, for instance; two deposits, four thousand dollars, held back with the story that she had loaned it to Timmy to buy a car. Now it seemed likely that she had put together the money herself for Timmy to take to the meeting with Devereaux.

And the story that he had gone to Toronto? Probably that had been agreed between them, although Marlow was already committed to spend the weekend with Pat Dakin, a circumstance he never bothered to tell his sister about. There was much else she didn't know, most of all, Timmy's real intention to kill Devereaux, probably with the same gun he had used seven years before. So Marlow had left his car in Dumpy Lake, rented another, and changed his appearance enough so he wouldn't be recognized at dusk when he came back to Larch River to wait for Devereaux. Caxton had been right about that, and Pickett would enjoy pointing it out to Wilkie at the appropriate moment. Marlow had four thousand in a paper sack, and a mistress waiting for him in a lodge by a lake. His only problem was Devereaux. He probably planned to kill Devereaux and dump the body in a gully in the bush, in a much deeper hole than the one Marlow's body was found in, and Pickett remembered that he had got this thought also from Caxton. He would let Wilkie know about that, too.

Marlow knew the area; with luck he could dispose of a body for good. No one would be looking for Devereaux in Larch River. He was just someone who had skipped parole a thousand miles away. Until Pickett had come along, even the car he had stolen was not connected to him. And nothing linked Devereaux with Marlow. The only connection would disappear with Devereaux's death. It was a perfect crime.

But Devereaux, presumably, after seven years in a penitentiary, was nobody's fall guy. Bailey had said he wasn't very bright, but he would have learned a few tricks in the penitentiary. He had a debt to collect; he had been loyal once and done Marlow a very big service, but he could not be sure how Marlow would respond to his request for gratitude. One of the possibilities, especially after the holdup, was that Marlow would try to pull something, and when he did, Devereaux would have seen it coming and probably killed Marlow while he was still taking the gun out of his pocket.

And then, as the train brought Pickett into Toronto, it was dusk, as it had been when Devereaux and Marlow met on the trail. Now it was Devereaux who had four thousand dollars. All he had to do was get to Sweetwater somehow and catch the bus to Toronto. What would have worked for Marlow would work for Devereaux, surely. No one would connect him with the dead Marlow. No one knew anything about him. He lived in Winnipeg, reporting regularly to his parole officer. All he had to do was get down to Toronto and catch a plane west with some of his money.

So why hadn't Devereaux done that? Had his nerve cracked? He was not a very experienced criminal, just someone who had been unlucky enough to try and rob a grocery store in company with a punk who had a gun.

Pickett took a cab from Union Station to his house, where he picked up his car and collected Willis from his next-door neighbor. The next morning he drove north, trying to concentrate on one problem at a time. He had some news for Wilkie that he ought to have phoned to him, bit by bit, as he uncovered it. His excuse was that until he learned that Devereaux had broken parole, he was just speculating, all begun with the curiosity about why Betty Cullen had falsified the date of her brother's arrival in town, seven years before. Pickett began to justify himself. He *had* told Wilkie he intended to respond to Mrs. Siggurdson. Wilkie had said, "Lotsa luck." Sort of mockingly. After that, one thing had led to another. At what point ought he to have called in? Surely not until now?

But he was still uneasy. What he had to tell Wilkie was that Marlow's killer was not in his cells, but somewhere on the loose, and with enough money to go to Tokyo if he wanted. Go get him, Wilkie. Lotsa luck. Jesus Christ. If only Devereaux had kept his head they could have picked him up at his next meeting with his parole officer. Why did he run? If it hadn't been for Mrs. Siggurdson, he would be sitting pretty.

Pickett stopped in Peterborough and spent a few hours eating lunch, buying some building supplies not available in Sweetwater, and generally postponing the meeting with Wilkie, because the more he thought about it, the more dissatisfied he became with his idea of what Devereaux had done after the shootout.

Coming into Larch River at sunset, Pickett drove down to the landing, parked, and walked up the trail to give Willis an airing before they went to the cabin. There was still just enough light to see the gully, and he tried to re-create the scene. With Marlow dead, surely Devereaux's first reaction would have been to hide, in case someone had heard the gunshot and come looking. Soon it would be dark, and Devereaux was in strange country. There was no point in crashing about the bush; he would not know about the concession road a quarter of a mile away, or how to get to it through the bush. He would have seen the cottages, though, on his way up the trail. So did he stay the night? Did he walk out on Saturday, risking being grabbed by the police, probably looking for the *lost* Marlow, or, at least, risking being noticed and identified later? Could he risk hitch-hiking the five miles into Sweetwater? Devereaux must have wondered if he had created a trap for himself.

Somebody could have heard the gun; for all he knew the search for the shooter would begin just as he emerged from the bush.

Pickett remembered that until Siggy had presented himself, Wilkie had done a pretty good job of questioning everybody in the area about any strangers they had seen, and all he had come up with was one man who had given a stranger a ride from Sweetwater to Larch River on the Friday, but no one who had seen or given a ride to anyone going the other way, on Friday, Saturday, or Sunday. And on Sunday, they had searched around the cottages, and Wilkie had posted cars to seal off the area. That was the point at which Pickett wondered if Devereaux was still nearby, and realized that he could be, bottled up by Wilkie.

In the very early morning, Pickett sat, with Willis on his lap, watching the light leach back into the sky like a stain spreading, and started at the other end. This time he thought about Betty Cullen, and her passion for respectability, how it had ended her future with Caxton, and probably condemned her to a lonely life as a shop assistant in Peterborough or somewhere. It was, he concluded again, nonsense, and he thought about the woman who doted on her brother so much that she had sacrificed her way of life for him, and her behavior since the death of her brother, and he wondered why she hadn't simply gone away for a while.

And then, thinking about Caxton, the image of the police chief sitting in his front window came to mind and he realized what Caxton had been doing, realized that he, Pickett, had been seeing the whole thing wrong, that it was like one of those optical puzzles where the foreground becomes the background as soon as you focus your eyes correctly.

As half a dozen details that he had brushed aside fell into place, Pickett became certain of his conclusion. The only problem left was Siggy, and Pickett got around Siggy by reminding himself that the man was a congenital liar with a dump truck for a lawyer.

What a lot he had to tell Wilkie.

For reasons that had to do with his upbringing about how to comport yourself on a formal occasion, he put on a clean pair of trousers and found a tie to wear over his workshirt, but he had no jacket except his windbreaker so he had to call on Wilkie looking like a Larch River native on his way to meet the bank manager. Like Wilkie, in fact.

CHAPTER 24

Wilkie greeted him cheerily, but Pickett tried to keep some formal distance between them to make it easier for Wilkie to get angry when Pickett had spoken his piece.

"I hear you were in Winnipeg," Wilkie said. "Did you find the guy you were looking for? Brendan! Come in here. I want you to hear this."

This should have warned him, but as well as being nervous about Wilkie's reaction, Pickett was still pleased with himself, and excited at what he was going to say. "Yes, Abe, I did."

"The bad guy, eh? Where's my pencil. I'll get his name down."

Copps entered and sat down, nodding to Pickett.

What the hell was going on? Wilkie's reaction was all wrong. These guys were practically winking at each other. But this was about finding a killer, not someone stealing newspapers. Wilkie was treating it as a routine event in a Sweetwater OPP morning.

Wilkie continued. "No. Don't tell me his name. Tell me the story first. How'd you get on to him?" To Copps he said, "Mel's found the killer. He's going to tell us how. That right, Mel? What got you started?"

233

"The dates," Pickett said finally. Was Wilkie sending him up? He looked quickly at Copps, who looked away. Something was going on, certainly. "The dates," he repeated. "I should tell you I think Betty Cullen knows a lot more than you thought."

"That right? What dates are these?"

Pickett explained, and Wilkie lost some of his air of mock wonder. Both policemen became more attentive. He had told them something they didn't know.

Starting from the discovery of the discrepancy over the dates of Marlow's arrival in Larch River, Pickett told his story, how he had tracked Marlow back to Winnipeg to the day he had left Winnipeg, and how he had discovered *why*, and uncovered Devereaux. Wilkie made no move now to write the name down. Pickett had all his attention as he described how Devereaux had probably stolen the car (here Wilkie looked at Copps, who started to make notes) and the circumstances of the meeting, backtracking now to Marlow's progress to the meeting that Friday, carrying the money his sister had given him.

"And Caxton?"

Pickett drew a breath. "I don't think he *knows* a thing."

"What's that mean?"

"I think he smells something, that's all."

"Go on." Now Wilkie was fascinated. "Tell us the rest. So what did you work on next?"

Again it was an odd response. Wilkie seemed to be more interested in the how than the what, in the teller than the tale. But Pickett's last two items should shift his interest. "So I asked myself how Devereaux could have disappeared so neatly, and why he hadn't turned up in Winnipeg."

Copps snorted and seemed to want to suppress a grin. Wilkie turned on him, furious. "Shut up. Shut the fuck up." He turned back to Pickett. "So what did you conclude, Sherlock?" But he was not being sarcastic. This time the wonder was real, admiring.

It was obvious that other dramas were being played out in the room, but Pickett's absorbed him totally. "That's when I realized, Abe," using the name to soften the bad news and associate himself with the sergeant, "that you've been looking for the wrong man. Devereaux's dead. It's Marlow you should be looking for."

Wilkie let out a sigh. Copps started to splutter, "You think we're totally . . ."

He got no further. Wilkie said sharply, "Leave us alone, Brendan." When Copps looked at him, amazed, he repeated, "Go on. Take a break. Before you go, though, you might congratulate this guy. You think you would have got there starting from where he did, without the help we had?"

Copps made a face, shrugged his shoulders, started to speak, then left the office, leaving the door open. Wilkie got up and closed it.

When Wilkie had sat down, Pickett said, "What's going on, Abe?"

Wilkie said, "You mind if we finish going over it first?"

"You don't seem very surprised."

"I'm not. I'll tell you why in a minute. Let's finish the

story. What happened? Marlow shot the Devereaux guy, then what?"

"Then he got disturbed by Siggy, maybe." Now Pickett stepped back from his second revelation. Whatever was going on with Wilkie and Copps, he could not believe they would be sitting here if they already knew what he was going to say next. So he waited. "I think he must have taken off, don't you?" he said. Actually he thought nothing of the kind. He watched for Wilkie's reaction. "So when did you know, and how did you get there?"

"Let's keep going," Wilkie said. "So Devereaux's dead, and Marlow is away, could be anywhere right now, right? Then along comes Siggy, finds a body, empties his wallet, and rolls him into the gully."

"Did he admit that? Disturbing the body?"

"He says it must have been bears. I say it was Siggy Goldilocks. I don't think it matters. He found Marlow's body on the trail. Then, on Sunday, the two lovers go for a walk and stumble over it, so to speak. Who was the next person to see the body, after them?"

"What is this? Caxton, when him and I went up the trail."

"He didn't get in there with Marlow's body, did he?"

"No."

"He recognized the jacket, right? Next we brought the ID out of that ditch, and took the body to the morgue here, and Betty Cullen identified it. Now what's going on? You say it was Devereaux. Would she have made a mistake like that?"

"No, she was lying. She knew all about Devereaux."

"From when?"

"From who, you mean."

"No, from when?"

"I don't know. Maybe from seven years ago. Maybe she knew all along, from the time that Marlow came to town and asked her for a place to hide. So when Devereaux came, she gave Marlow the money to make him go away. She didn't expect Marlow to kill him, but when he did she still tried to look after him. The trouble is, it makes more sense if she only just found out, like, last week. She was making plans with Lyman. She wouldn't have done that if she had been expecting someone like Devereaux to show up for the last seven years, would she?"

"Okay. Then?"

"Marlow came back to the bakery in a panic, and she agreed to help. Even now, Caxton still didn't have to be involved. You remember she got flu and wouldn't let him in."

"So did he know or not?"

"I don't know. No, he didn't."

"But Betty knew."

"Oh, sure. She knew."

"Okay, Mel. Now let's see if you can answer your own question. Who else saw Marlow's body?"

"Siggy. He's my problem. He knew Marlow, all right, so he'd know this guy wasn't him. Marlow hadn't been mauled at that point, though I understand his face was smashed in. But it wouldn't have been enough. From the pictures I've seen, Devereaux and Marlow were of an age, and about the same size, but they weren't all that much alike. Siggy must have known, but he figured he was better off lying. Maybe he saw a chance of black-mailing Marlow down the road, if he could ever find him when he came out of jail."

Wilkie nodded and breathed out loudly. "Simpler than that. He knew, all right. For him it was just a legitimate body to rob, somebody he had never seen in his life before, so he proceeded to rob it. Then, when he heard they'd found Marlow dead, he couldn't exactly rush in here and tell us who it really was, could he? We had to wait until we charged him with homicide. Then he told us."

Then Pickett saw the whole game. "So he told you, but you didn't tell the world, right?"

Wilkie nodded, savoring the moment.

"When? When did he tell you? Before I left town?"

"That's right."

"So when you told me he was pleading guilty, that was all bullshit, right?"

"That was for the benefit of Marlow, make him think we'd wrapped up the case. I couldn't risk telling anyone a different story. Not even you, Mel."

"So you knew for a week what I was going to find, if I found it."

"Four days. I did try to warn you, you were wasting your time."

"What a laugh you've had. So why aren't you looking for Marlow?"

"I am. But I've got the okay to leave it off the com-puter for a few days."

"Why?"

"Caxton has a computer."

"So what the hell *are* you doing? Seems to me you're just sitting here feeling smug about the fact that Siggy told you how wrong you were. You haven't done fuck-all, have you?"

But Wilkie was a hard man to rile. "I'm waiting, that's what I'm doing. Look at it like this. We know that Marlow killed this guy, and that his sister knows, but nobody else does. Everybody else thinks we're looking for Marlow's killer."

"In the meantime, Marlow could be in New Zealand by now."

"I doubt it." Wilkie smiled. "Marlow doesn't have any money."

"Four thousand dollars?"

"He doesn't have it."

"How do you know that? Of course. Siggy."

"Siggy remembered where the money was after we'd made him into some kind of informer and he'd seen what a difference it made to how we looked for Marlow. Siggy had stashed it under one of the cottages, after lifting out a handful of fifties, I would suspect. But knowing Marlow doesn't have it is more important than proving Siggy stole it, so we are going to tell everybody that we found it."

"Don't let him off too lightly, will you? I don't like being told to fuck off by a scumbag like that."

"He's an informer. They're all scumbags."

"Let's get back to the story. You've got Marlow without any money and therefore not too far away. Now, what did you decide Marlow did next?"

"What do you think?"

"This is your story now. I want to hear how *you* made an asshole of yourself."

Wilkie smiled. "I think we'll look okay. Marlow's hiding somewhere, but his only source of money is Betty. I've got a bug on that bakery phone, so all I have to do is wait. When he calls, and Betty goes to meet him, or conceivably when he's feeling real cocky and comes in himself when he thinks it's safe, we'll pick him up."

My turn, Pickett thought. My turn, Wilkie, old son. "He hasn't called yet?"

"No."

"Ten days. And no money. A little strange?"

"He's got whatever money Devereaux had on him."

"Devereaux was on welfare, and he had to steal a car to get out here. Devereaux didn't have any money on him."

"Look, Mel, I don't have an answer for everything. I admit he's been out there a long time, but he thinks we think he's dead. So he thinks he can walk around free as long as he stays away from this area. But he's going to have to call for help soon."

"How long are you going to wait?"

"My boss likes the scheme."

"And Siggy?"

"He's tickled to be a part of it. He has to stay in jail, but he gets extra privileges. Half a Coke bottle of rye before supper."

"Nice." Pickett leaned forward. "It won't work, though."

"Why?"

"Because Marlow isn't out there."

And Pickett told him where he was.

Wilkie absorbed the information very quickly. "Has to be," he agreed. He laughed. "Let me get Brendan in. You can tell him yourself." He laughed again. "Brendan!" he called. "Come in here. Mel's got something he wants to share with you."

As they reached the bakery, Pickett pointed down the street to Caxton's house. "You going to leave Lyman out of this?"

Wilkie considered. "He knows the layout of the house, doesn't he?"

"Yes, and I think he's been watching it for a week. He got there first. He's been waiting for him."

Wilkie thought about this, nodded, and continued on to Caxton's house. When he told Caxton the mission, all Caxton said was "Let's go, then. I was just waiting for him to poke his head out, so I could break it off."

CHAPTER 25

After they had gone through the ground floor and the bedrooms, Caxton opened the trapdoor to the cellar to find Marlow waiting on the top stair, waving his gun. There was ten days' growth of beard on his face, which might have allowed him to be spirited away at night, now that Siggy was in jail and no one was looking hard for strangers anymore. Caxton ignored the gun and kicked Marlow in the face and jumped through the hole after him, using him to cushion his landing.

"Here," Wilkie called, and threw down a pair of handcuffs. Caxton put the cuffs in his pocket and kicked Marlow ahead of him, up the stairs. Marlow came through the trapdoor and sprawled onto the floor. As he was getting to his knees, Caxton kicked him in the ribs. "Up, buddy," he said, and as Marlow tried to stagger upright, kicked him again to point him toward the door.

Wilkie, who had been watching with some detachment, said, "Put him in the car. And don't kick him again."

"Just one more," Caxton said. "I don't like people pointing guns at me. Especially him. Let's go, hero."

Wilkie sprang suddenly to his feet to get between Caxton and Marlow. "That's enough," he said. "You hear?" He pushed Caxton away. "Get over there," he ordered him. "I'll take care of this man." He put an arm around Marlow's shoulders. "You okay? Let's get out to the car."

When the door closed, Caxton looked at Pickett in surprise. "Did I do something wrong? The guy had a gun."

Pickett laughed. "You played your part perfectly. Now it's Wilkie's turn. He's cute. Quick, too."

An hour later, Copps had taken Betty Cullen to Sweetwater to be charged. Wilkie returned to the bakery, assigning two constables to escort Marlow away. Wilkie stayed to talk to Pickett, telling Copps to send a car back in an hour to pick him up at the coffee shop.

Charlotte, smelling the excitement, sparkling a little with it, put coffee in front of them and moved almost out of earshot.

"You first," Wilkie said. "Start at the end. How did you know he was in the cellar?"

"I knew he was in the house and there was no sign of him aboveground. She never closed the curtains in the bedrooms or downstairs, and there was never a face at the window."

"You watched from the street."

"No, Lyman did that. I remembered noticing. Afterward. When I was in Sweetwater, visiting you so that Betty could identify the body, she asked me to stop for groceries, so that she wouldn't have to talk to anyone while she was shopping in Larch River, she said. She came out of the IGA with three sacks of groceries. For one person. This was the first week after the body turned up. And I noticed her going into the hardware store here in Larch River, and the drugstore, and keeping up a pretty good chat with everyone she bumped into. Then there was the fact that she didn't reopen the bakery. I thought she'd close it for a day and then again the day of the funeral. Isn't that normal? But the sign's still up; she never did reopen. You know the reason? She had no one to bring up the sacks of flour from the cellar. Caxton did it for a while, after her husband died and before Timmy showed up. It's how they got to know each other, so he'd know they're too heavy for her. If Caxton was in on it, he could've brought up the flour. No one would've thought anything of that."

"She didn't want us to touch Caxton. Said he didn't know anything about it. I see what you mean by saying he smelled something. He knew it subconsciously, I think."

"This is fancy stuff, Abe. This is psychology, is it? Police college stuff? How does it go over in Sweetwater?"

"Go fuck yourself. Where were you at?"

"Yeah, so she bought her groceries in Sweetwater, and everything else in Larch River. She kept the bakery closed. So I figured, or rather, it came to me this morning, that she didn't want anyone to see that she was still buying groceries for two people. And she couldn't open the bakery because Timmy was there somewhere and she couldn't risk someone wandering around the house and shop. The idea that she couldn't bring the flour up just came to me. See, if Timmy had brought up the flour

244

at night, she would have to tell Lyman Caxton that it was the fairies or something."

"Don't go overboard. Remind me now when and how you knew it was Devereaux who was dead, not Marlow."

"Did *you* know it was Devereaux? The actual Paul Devereaux?"

"We'd have got there. I didn't care who it was. What I knew was that it wasn't Marlow, so Marlow was the guy I was looking for."

"Siggy told you."

"Right, right. I didn't cleverly figure it out, and relying on Siggy, I could've screwed up. Okay? Write it out and I'll sign it. Okay? Now. Your turn."

"When I found Devereaux had disappeared for no good reason it seemed a natural fit. The logical thing for Devereaux to have done was shoot back to Winnipeg, although rounders aren't always logical."

"What started you off on the trail again?"

"Betty Cullen lying about the date Timmy came to town. She had to be covering, even now, something that happened just before he arrived. Something that happened in Winnipeg, most likely. When the store owner was shot."

"And the rest was simple. Even I could have done it."

"You didn't have to. You cheated. You had Siggy."

"I should have told you. Could have saved you a lot of trouble."

"I enjoyed it. I got to ride the train again. So what did Marlow have to say? More coffee, Charlotte, please?" Pickett wanted to savor this story.

"The whole thing?"

"From Winnipeg seven years ago. By the way, I've never seen the friendly cop trick done better. Did you sit him on your lap? Did he cry?"

"Just about."

"Caxton couldn't figure out what you were doing."

"It's not in the manual. So, back in Winnipeg, seven years ago, two pals robbed a convenience store. These two knew each other from before, as you found out, met up again in a beer parlor, both broke, and Marlow had the idea of a quick smash-and-grab. You found out the rest. So Marlow spent a few days waiting for the cops to come, then realized that Devereaux hadn't fingered him. When he realized he'd got away with it, he came east to settle down with his sister. He figured that as long as he stayed around Winnipeg, there was always a chance that some cop would ask him where he was when the store owner got shot."

"Did she know?"

"He had to tell her because she didn't want to take him in. When she heard what he'd done, she decided to cover him."

"It wasn't just that she doted on him."

"Okay, okay, there was nothing going on there, sure. But then Devereaux got released and called Marlow for money. Personally I think he might have had something going for Marlow, keeping quiet like that, serving extra time and all."

Pickett sighed. "Jesus Christ. You're as bad as your buddy."

Wilkie grinned. "I mean it was Marlow bringing along a gun in the first place that landed Devereaux in it. He had no idea of shooting anyone in that convenience store. But when Marlow didn't send him any money, Devereaux came looking for him."

"How did he know where to look?"

"I asked him about that. Marlow told him, at that fishing camp. They were sort of buddies, and Marlow told him all about his sister. Even Devereaux could guess that Marlow had probably run here. So he called the bakery from Winnipeg, and sure enough Marlow answered the phone. So Devereaux came east. He called again from Sweetwater, and Marlow told him to meet him on the trail. Marlow told his sister he was being blackmailed and she put together the money. This is where her brother got cute. As you guessed, he planned to kill Devereaux, drop him in one of the holes in the bush like the one we found him in, and keep the money. No one knew he was there, and even if they found him, no one would connect him with Marlow."

"So what happened?"

"Siggy. Siggy was wandering around the woods, and he heard a shot. So, after a while he went to take a look at who was target-shooting when it was nearly dark. Marlow was just getting organized to haul Devereaux away when he heard Siggy coming through the bush, so he dropped Devereaux and lay back to watch. Siggy found the bag of money, saw the body, shouted out "Timmy" to see if it would move, went to take a look, rolled it over, then ran.

"Now Marlow had to figure out what Siggy would do next. Probably nothing. Siggy had four thousand in a paper sack, and the longer it took them to find the body the farther away Siggy could arrange to be. Siggy headed home, of course, trying to look as if he'd never left. But Marlow has no real way of knowing what Siggy would do. He's panicking. He waited a couple of hours and nothing happened, then he starts to think. When he puts it all together he realizes that Siggy never got a good look at the body, he just assumed it was Marlow because the money was in a bag with the bakery's name on it. So Marlow thinks that Siggy thinks that the body is his, and if that's the case, he's going to be surprised if Marlow appears in town. At any rate, the money will keep Siggy quiet, so Marlow changes his plan. He stuffs his wallet in Devereaux's pocket, puts his wristwatch on him, and his jacket, shoots him in the face again, probably, and rolls him into the crevasse, and kicks a lot of leaves over him.

"Now he's committed. It isn't safe for him to take the rented car back to Dumpy Lake. There's only one safe thing to do, disappear. With any luck, and if he judged Siggy right, they might not find the body for a long time; a week would be enough with the plan he had in mind now. Point is, no one would miss him for a couple of days. He thought they'd never trace the car in the shed back to him, except that the asshole left the stolen ID in his wallet, which he left on Devereaux's body. So once more Betty Cullen took him in. In a week or so, she was going to drive him to Peterborough, with enough money so he could disappear.

"It was full of holes, of course, but it might have worked. Don't forget the essentials: officially we have a dead Marlow in the morgue, identified by his sister.

We're supposed to be looking for his killer still." Wilkie laughed. "When he heard they'd charged Siggy, he thought he was home free. But Siggy was mine."

"You didn't need Siggy. I'd've helped you out, eventually. What about Betty Cullen?"

"She was going to sell the bakery and move. He told her when Devereaux showed up. She gave him the money, but when he came back, telling her he'd killed Devereaux, she took him in and hid him in the basement. Gave up her whole life on the spot."

Pickett nodded. He was thinking about Caxton. It had come to him that dawn, when he realized what Caxton reminded him of. Once in Toronto he had suffered from mice, so he had bought a cat, and he'd had the familiar experience of seeing the cat wait forever by a hole for a mouse to appear. That morning, as he was trying to think about the last steps in the story, he had realized that Caxton had been sitting in his own window, with a view of the bakery, all night and every night as far as Pickett could tell, ever since that Sunday. What Pickett had worked out eventually, putting all the little clues like the grocery shopping together, Caxton must have felt instinctively, smelled it out by the way the house looked and by the way his girlfriend acted. But he had been planning to handle Marlow personally.

"What about Lyman Caxton? What's going to happen to him?" he wondered.

"He followed them into Sweetwater. He said he had to look after her."

"I guess this'll be your bailiwick now."

"How's that?"

"They won't replace Lyman. They'll contract Larch River out to you guys."

"When's my turn?" Charlotte poured more coffee into his cup. "When am I going to hear what happened at the bakery so I won't have to wait for all the customers to tell me?"

"Tonight?"

"Come up to the house."

"Tonight?"

"Eat your supper here, and we'll go up when I close. Your girl friend was in looking for you. Eliza."

"What did she want?"

"Something about the play must go on and she's staying here to finish it. They are thinking of having it ready by Christmas. But she hasn't been able to find another place to live. She could stay where she is in the trailer until Christmas, couldn't she?"

"There's no heat. It'll get pretty cold in a month. But sure. I'll tell her."

By eleven o'clock he had told her the story. He got up to go home. She stayed seated on the couch. As he reached the door, she said, "Why can't you stay here?" The tone of her voice was that of a child asking why she can't be allowed to do the pleasant thing for a change, instead of the unpleasant other.

"I could stay here. Nothing to stop me."

"Then stay here. Sleep here."

"You don't mind?"

"What am I saying?"

250

He sat down. "Let's have a drink. You, too."

She shook her head, but he went into the kitchen and found her half bottle of scotch under the skirt of the doll and poured himself a large one. He returned to the living room and sat down beside her and put his arm around her. She stiffened, shivered, and collapsed lightly against him, head resting against the side of his chest. He leaned over awkwardly and kissed her near the top of her ear.

"Marry me," he said.

"Sure. But you don't have to."

"Yes, I do. I didn't think we'd get to the point. But we're there now."

"You are."

"Aren't you?"

"I've been there awhile."

All of the questions were set aside now in a spontaneous request. The whole debate he had been solemnly putting himself through, preparing for this day, or not, depending how the debate went; weighing the advantages of the renewed pleasure of bed, board, and most of all, companionship, against the disadvantages; all the decisions that would have to be made (he had recently sworn he would never move house again); the rules that would have to be laid down, for example, to point out in words that he had reached sixty-five without a beer belly or heart disease so he would eat and drink what he liked because he was naturally abstemious, apparently, and having come this far he might as well finish off his life with butter, too, because he didn't like margarine. All this was set aside now in the discovery on his tongue of the words "Marry me." And her response had reminded him that maybe there was more motive in his asking the question now; he had probably sensed that it was in her head, and for once he wanted to have the initiative, to exercise the male prerogative while it still existed. She could have all the others.

"We have to decide where we'll live," he said.

"I've been thinking about that. I don't want to stay here all winter anymore. I'd like to sell this house and put together a decent . . ."

"Dowry?"

". . . income of my own. We'll be well fixed."

Charlotte's first husband had been an insurance salesman and a real estate agent and he had left her enough life insurance to live on and a mortgage-free house. She continued, "I was thinking, we could live in your cabin in the summer, after I've fixed it up a bit, until Christmas, maybe, because it's nice in the country till then. Then we could move back to your house in Toronto until late April or early May. You like to go to Florida, I know, and to Europe. I'll come to Florida, but you can go to Europe on your own. I don't much like being a tourist anymore."

"What about your job?"

"It's time to quit. I told Harlan I wouldn't stay on much longer, he should start looking for someone else. He'd like me to keep helping out during the summer. I could do that, I think."

"In the meantime, I could move in here and Eliza can have the cabin. Just until Christmas. Shall I? Move in here?"

"I wish you would."